POISONOUS WORDS

"Mr. Stokes," I said. Harry's son didn't seem to hear me but kept shouting, repeating himself without winding down.

Finally, he stopped shouting and looked directly at me. "You're not helping; you're part of the problem!"

"Mr. Stokes, last night I spent two hours at police headquarters going over the prescription records of your late father, Betsy Stokes, and others. I suggest you see Detective Moreway and discuss all this with him."

His expression became even more filled with hatred. If he had a weapon, I was sure he'd use it, and I was prepared to drop to the Mexican tile floor behind the prescription counter. "Maybe we've been suspecting the wrong person," he said. "After all, you have more access to poisons than anyone else!"

Avon Books are available at special quantity discounts for bulk purchases for sales promotions, premiums, fund raising or educational use. Special books, or book excerpts, can also be created to fit specific needs.

For details write or telephone the office of the Director of Special Markets, Avon Books, Dept. FP, 1350 Avenue of the Americas, New York, New York 10019, 1-800-238-0658.

Rx FOR MURDER

RENEE B. HOROWITZ

AVON BOOKS • NEW YORK

VISIT OUR WEBSITE AT
http://AvonBooks.com

Excerpt from "The Folly of Being Comforted" from *The Poems of W. B. Yeats: A New Edition,* edited by Richard Finneran (New York: Macmillan, 1983).

RX FOR MURDER is an original publication of Avon Books. This work has never before appeared in book form. This work is a novel. Any similarity to actual persons or events is purely coincidental.

AVON BOOKS
A division of
The Hearst Corporation
1350 Avenue of the Americas
New York, New York 10019

Copyright © 1997 by Renee B. Horowitz
Published by arrangement with the author
Library of Congress Catalog Card Number: 96-96483
ISBN: 0-380-78619-2

All rights reserved, which includes the right to reproduce this book or portions thereof in any form whatsoever except as provided by the U.S. Copyright Law. For information address Thompson and Chris Literary Agency, 16 Castellain Mansions, Castellain Road, London, W9 1HA England.

First Avon Books Printing: January 1997

AVON TRADEMARK REG. U.S. PAT. OFF. AND IN OTHER COUNTRIES, MARCA REGISTRADA, HECHO EN U.S.A.

Printed in the U.S.A.

RA 10 9 8 7 6 5 4 3 2 1

If you purchased this book without a cover, you should be aware that this book is stolen property. It was reported as "unsold and destroyed" to the publisher, and neither the author nor the publisher has received any payment for this "stripped book."

To my husband, Arthur Horowitz, Registered Pharmacist
and to the memories of both our dads:
Hyman Braunstein, Registered Pharmacist
and Sam M. Horowitz, Registered Pharmacist

ACKNOWLEDGMENTS

Many thanks to Kathi George, Janice Steinberg,
Teresa Chris, and Lyssa Keusch

Author's Note

To the best of my knowledge, there is no supermarket chain called Food Go. I also coined the name Food-Fed for the store brand of a decongestant that plays an important part in this story. Rogaine, the hair regrowth treatment, no longer requires a prescription but now can be bought "over the counter," as can Nicoderm, the nicotine patch.

One that is ever kind said yesterday:
"Your well-belovèd's hair has threads of grey,
And little shadows come about her eyes;
Time can but make it easier to be wise
Though now it seems impossible, and so
All that you need is patience."

    Heart cries, "No,
I have not a crumb of comfort, not a grain.
Time can but make her beauty over again:
Because of that great nobleness of hers
The fire that stirs about her, when she stirs,
Burns but more clearly. O she had not these ways
When all the wild summer was in her gaze."

O heart! O heart! if she'd but turn her head,
You'd know the folly of being comforted.

> "The Folly of Being Comforted"
> William Butler Yeats

One

Five customers were waiting at the pharmacy window, and Joey had gone on break. I needed a break, too, but there was no way I could leave.

"Miss, when will the pharmacist be back?" A woman about my own age peered through the window at me. She wore a bright paisley blouse with clashing pink shorts and pink tennis shoes.

"I'm the pharmacist," I said. "May I help you?" My smile was forced. I could see she wouldn't accept me as a professional, but, I reminded myself, it was worse thirty years ago when I got my pharmacy degree.

"No, I mean the fellow who just left. The pharmacist."

She was ready to believe that Joey Franklin, my twenty-year-old technician, was in charge. "I'm the pharmacist," I repeated more firmly, straightening the lapels of my white lab jacket so she could read the words on the name tag: RUTH KANTOR MORRIS, PHARMACY MANAGER. She never looked at it but did hand over two prescriptions.

While I tried to clear the backlog, more people lined up at the window. I waved and said, "Be with you in a minute," but one waiting customer walked away. People want instantaneous service today. I try not to let it bother me when I lose business for my company, Food Go, but it's frustrating. And not just because I'm in the employee stock plan.

It was hot even with the air conditioner blasting away. Summertime, I wear my hair short to cope with the desert heat, but my forehead was uncomfortably damp. With the back of one hand, I brushed a lock of auburn hair, tinted nowadays, out of the way and rushed to help more waiting customers.

Joey returned from his break and pitched in. His dark eyes, always sharply intelligent, seemed animated with suppressed excitement, but we couldn't talk until a pause in the flow of customers about an hour later.

"Do you remember that old guy who comes in for his Oreton? The one with the pretty blond wife." He waited while I handed out a prescription and cautioned the customer not to take it with dairy products. "You always say that's why widows like you don't have a chance. Because the old guys marry young gals. . . . I didn't really mean *old*." Joey looked stricken.

I remembered him all right. Harry Stokes. Another one who thought male hormones like Oreton would help him keep a young wife. "Was he in for a refill today? It can't be more than a few days since the last time."

Joey's excitement was at the bursting point. "He won't need Oreton now."

"What happened?" I asked.

"He's dead."

I felt a pang of sadness. Harry Stokes had been good-looking and polite. I always remembered the polite customers. And I appreciated the way he respected my professional judgment—often asking my opinion about nonprescription drugs.

Someone was tapping on the pharmacy window to get my attention. I looked up.

"Excuse me. Where's the rubbers?" It was a teenage girl.

"Just over there, on the left." In my day, women never bought condoms, and certainly girls didn't. Even men were embarrassed to ask for them. Thirty years ago, they'd come into Dad's store and wait for me to walk away from the counter. After a while, I learned to busy myself elsewhere so they could talk to Dad alone.

A customer left three new prescriptions at the window, and I had no time to question Joey further. Joey looked like he wanted to say more but had to get the phone, one call right after the other. He was a dependable technician, who wanted to study medicine someday, and was always asking questions. Although pharmacy law required me to check his work, I rarely found an error.

By the time Joey's shift ended, half a dozen people were waiting for their medications, and I barely had a chance to wave goodbye to him. I had no opportunity at all to think of Harry Stokes.

But I like to keep busy, and the night schedule works best for me since Bob died. It's that much later till I have to go back to my empty house. Nearly two years, but I still can't get used to being alone. My friends tell me, "Come on, Ruthie. It's not like you can't manage. You're different than the other women of our generation. Most of us didn't have careers."

Then they talk on, letting me know how lucky I am to have a profession, to have always worked, to make a good salary, to have no children. I stopped communicating my feelings and fears after the first bewildered months of loneliness. No one wants to hear the truth, anyhow. They ask, "How are you, Ruthie?" and I say, "Fine." And most of the time, I am fine.

I guess it's getting better because I don't cry myself to sleep very often anymore. And about a year ago, I started noticing good-looking men like Harry Stokes. He was a little older than Bob, and his expression wasn't as serious. Bob always seemed to be working out a problem in his head, maybe because of his engineering background. Friends considered me the outgoing one and Bob the introvert. But then again, I deal with people all day long, and he worked with machines.

Don't misunderstand me! Nothing was the matter with Bob's sense of humor. Sometimes it seemed to take him forever to get to the punch line of a joke, but I'd give anything to hear him tell one again. I wouldn't get impatient either.

Harry Stokes was different. He smiled more and he kidded with Joey or with me whenever he came in. Not about the Oreton, though. We didn't dare joke about hormones.

I knew he'd been a widower for some years because Denise Seaford from the Food Go coffee shop had pointed him out to me. Denise was a divorcée, about ten years younger than me, and she was interested in Harry Stokes. She lived next door to Harry and knew all about him. In fact, I remember the day last October when Denise told me he remarried.

"She's after his money."

I laughed. Denise thrived on melodrama. "After all the times you've told me how much you like him," I said. "Maybe she feels the same way."

"That's different. I'm old enough to appreciate a man in his sixties. But she's only half his age." Then Denise leaned over my table and spoke softly, as if confiding a secret. "She's just a couple of years older than his children. Could be the same age as the married son, now that I think of it."

Denise had to leave to refill someone's coffee. My shift in the Food Go pharmacy over, I sat there thinking about Harry Stokes and his young wife. I had never told Denise that I sometimes daydreamed about Harry. He'd see me standing behind the pharmacy window, nibbling on some danish and gulping down coffee between customers.

"Let me take you to dinner," he'd say. "You look like you need to relax."

"Wonderful idea," I'd answer. My imagination worked very well with the details: what I would wear, when he would call for me, where we would eat, and what we would say to each other. We'd find that we laughed together and talked a lot. I could work out the conversation in the restaurant, but after that my imagination faltered. It had been too many years since I'd dated, if they even called it that today. I had no idea how to act after dinner or whether Harry, who was from my generation, would expect me to be uninhibited like the younger women I talk to and read about. Well, now I knew. He had skipped a generation in choosing a new wife.

Denise returned and started to tell me that her neighbors all figured the Stokes children were unhappy about the marriage. "When so many years went by and he didn't remarry, the kids thought they were safe."

"Safe?"

"It's like a TV soap. There's money. Lots of money. And the son and daughter are used to having whatever they want."

I thought Denise was probably exaggerating. Most of the young people I know want their divorced or widowed parents to remarry. That way, they don't have to worry about them. Or if they're less selfish, they want the parents to be happy.

Denise went away again to microwave a slice of pizza for someone. When she came back, we occupied ourselves comparing schedules. We were looking for a night when we were both off and could go to the movies together.

Since then she'd kept me up to date about Harry Stokes and his wife, Betsy. I knew they honeymooned on Maui, and I heard when they redecorated Harry's home. Denise told me Betsy was pretty, but a stereotypical dumb blonde. "And you should see her clothes. She never wears the same thing twice."

"How do you know?" In Scottsdale, we don't see much of our neighbors. We all live behind our block fences and, although we spend a lot of time outdoors, it's usually on our own patios or in our own swimming pools.

"I see her getting into her BMW, the new one he bought for her. Or walking out to the mailbox."

Denise seemed envious. I knew she was struggling, even though she had kept her house as part of the divorce settlement. Not for the first time, I thought what a nice bit of gossip it would make for Denise if she learned that Harry Stokes was taking Oreton, the male hormone drug. But of course I wouldn't reveal anything about a customer's prescriptions.

Now, instead of the details of Harry's new life with Betsy Stokes, I would be hearing about his death and funeral. I shivered and began my closing procedure for the pharmacy.

I connected the order machine to the telephone and began to transmit forty or fifty items from the order book. The pharmacy closed at nine, although Food Go stayed open all night. That made it hard to get out of the place, because last-minute customers could come into the store while I tried to finish up. Sure enough, while I was printing a copy of my computer's Rx record for the day, a woman came in with a prescription for birth control pills.

"Why couldn't she get here sooner," I grumbled to myself as I filled her prescription. "They never remember until they start to think about bed."

At least I didn't have to back up the entire day's prescriptions the way they did in some pharmacies. All Food Go stores were linked to a mainframe computer at the central office, and they ran the backups.

I took off my white jacket, put it neatly on a hanger, locked the door to the pharmacy, and went to sign out. Yes, we have to punch a time card even though we're supposed to be professionals. That's one disadvantage of working for a chain of supermarkets. Dad would have been upset if he'd lived long enough to see me working for Food Go. I remember the bitterness in his voice whenever he talked about the "chains" and the way their competition was forcing him out of business.

Thinking about Dad and how pharmacy has changed over the years, I reached in my handbag for the canister of Mace that I always carry, and walked out of the store. Employees are supposed to park at the outer perimeter of the lot and leave the closer spaces for customers. And although the Food Go parking lot is well lit, occasionally there are assaults and carjackings around town. It doesn't hurt to be careful.

Just as I pulled into my driveway, I remembered I'd wanted to look up Harry Stokes's prescription record. I was curious to see what other medications he'd been taking.

Two

When I work nights, I often have lunch in the Food Go coffee shop before signing in. On Tuesday I got there early enough to visit with Denise. Always ready to say what was uppermost on her mind, she began speaking even before I pulled out one of the green plastic-covered chairs and picked up a menu.

"Did you hear about Harry Stokes?"

I mumbled the usual sympathetic words, trying to discern at the same time if Denise looked the way she always did. Despite the heat, her makeup had been carefully applied. As usual, her eye shadow, lavender today, dramatically emphasized pale gray eyes. I saw no sign of tears or a sleepless night, and her makeup wasn't heavy enough to hide any traces of emotional outpouring for Harry Stokes. But I couldn't interpret the slight difference I did read in her expression.

After that quick glance to assess Denise's reactions, my first thought was a selfish one: good, she wasn't really in love with him. I don't have to treat her like a mourner.

Denise leaned over the table to take my order and retrieve the menu, although we both knew that I always had the same tuna salad and sun tea at this time of the year. We were in the middle of the Arizona monsoon season, with temperatures hovering at the 110-degree mark and unusually high humidity. But under pretense of taking the order, she could spend more time talking to me.

"You'll never believe what's happening," she said. "The children want an autopsy."

I stared at her, startled at the news. She smoothed the frilly green apron that served more to identify her as a Food Go waitress than to protect her clothes. Denise, always immaculate no matter how busy the coffee shop was, wore a multicolored, slightly flared skirt in shades of violet, orchid, and lavender. Her sleeveless blouse picked up the same lavender as the skirt, both exactly one shade darker than her eye shadow. Although Denise was no taller than my own five and a half feet, with hair the color we used to call dirty blond, she made me feel nondescript in my pale yellow shirtdress.

Denise clearly enjoyed my surprise. "Betsy won't allow it. Don't you think that's suspicious?"

"You've been reading too many Sue Graftons," I said. "Any wife would be distraught at the idea of an autopsy. I was terrified they'd insist on one for Bob."

"That's different. You told me you couldn't allow an autopsy for religious reasons."

"Even so," I said. "An autopsy's the last thing a new widow wants to think about."

A young couple in matching khaki shorts and T-shirts advertising a walkathon went to a table at the opposite end of the coffee shop. While Denise waited on them, I thought about autopsies. Didn't the need for one simply mean the cause of death hadn't been clearly established?

It was just like Denise to dramatize everyday events. Well, maybe a neighbor's death wasn't exactly an everyday event, especially a neighbor she'd wanted. And you, I asked myself, weren't you also looking at him that way? But I told myself that was different, because I'd never mentioned my daydreams to anyone; they served only to pass the time.

I was still thinking about those daydreams, unwillingly comparing them to reality, when Denise returned with my sun tea. "Why do people always sit as far away from each other as they can?" she asked. But she was smiling when she said it. Denise never got upset with her customers, even the demanding ones, and I often wished I had her patience.

I didn't comment. I was more interested in the Harry Stokes drama than where people chose to sit in Food Go's coffee shop. "Do his children suspect murder?"

Again, I saw something indefinably different in her expression. "Now, who reads too many mysteries?" she asked me.

Although we were talking about the death of someone we both cared about, I found myself grinning at Denise. "It's a natural question. Why else would they want an autopsy?"

"They claim she drove their dad to suicide."

"Suicide!"

"It's not as farfetched as murder."

"Yes, but it seems unlikely when they'd been married such a short time."

"I don't know about that," Denise muttered before she left to take care of her other customers.

I sat there, sipping my sun tea and thinking about Denise's comments. Would a seemingly well-balanced man like Harry Stokes commit suicide? What if he remarried and then discovered he'd made a mistake? Even though Arizona is a community-property state, divorce seemed more likely. Denise had told me Harry Stokes was wealthy. Surely, he would have insisted on a prenuptial agreement to protect his children.

Denise returned with my tuna sandwich and I told her what I'd been thinking. "Some people don't want to look foolish," she said.

"Suicide is a rather drastic way to avoid looking foolish." But as I ate, I remembered Harry Stokes's prescriptions for Rogaine and Oreton. Surely a man who was planning suicide wouldn't be getting refills to control baldness and increase his sex drive. I'd have to look up the computer records and see when we'd last filled those scripts.

My watch showed that it was time to get going. I paid for lunch, lost the battle of the tip again—Denise always refused to accept one from me—and went to punch my time card with five minutes to spare.

Tim Barnard, my staff pharmacist, was working the day shift. He was planted at the computer while Joey took care of customers at the window, answered the telephone, and handled the cash register. I knew from experience that Tim would not move away from the computer unless I forced the issue. He considered it an assault on his professionalism to touch the telephone or the register, and didn't like talking to customers unless he had to.

I got a "Thank God, you're here" look from Joey and a shrug in Tim's direction. Tim, about a dozen years older than the technician and a registered pharmacist, didn't treat Joey very well. For that matter, he was often obnoxious to me, too. He'd been with us about a year, and Joey and I both wished he'd never transferred from a Food Go pharmacy in Tucson.

The day's order from our drug warehouse had come in but wasn't unpacked. I knew better than to expect help from Tim, so I asked Joey to begin while I took over the window. Between customers and phone calls, I went back and worked with Joey.

"You'll never believe what's happening," he said, echoing Denise. He seemed even more disturbed than she had been, but maybe he was just excited about the unusual situation. I wondered if I seemed different, too.

"I know. The Stokes children want an autopsy."

Joey deflated. "Oh, you had lunch in the coffee shop and Denise told you."

I admitted this was true and repeated my reaction to Denise's suppositions. The phone rang five or six times, ignored by Tim, who didn't seem to pay attention to our conversation either. He, at least, was acting the way he always did.

Since I was the responsible pharmacist, I picked up the phone and took down a Vicodin Rx from a local dentist. I handed it to Tim at the computer.

"Someone ought to report that dentist to the State Board," Tim grumbled. "He prescribes too many narcotics for his patients."

Tim was probably right, but I didn't say anything. He complained enough without encouragement. I returned to the back of the pharmacy to work with Joey, who had already unpacked and priced out the over-the-counter items. "Thanks for finishing the OTCs," I said to him.

"But I've been waiting to tell you the really great news. My brother-in-law is working on the Stokes case." Joey's excitement surfaced again.

"How can it be a case if it was a natural death?"

"That's what they're trying to find out. And I'll be in on all the details because of Frank."

Joey's older sister was married to someone on the Scottsdale police force. I hadn't really paid much attention when he'd talked about Frank Moreway and the cases he was on. Dad had so imbued me with the necessity for professional discretion that I found it difficult to understand people who gossiped about privileged information.

"You must never repeat anything you hear behind this counter," Dad told me long before I entered pharmacy college. "You'll learn who's pregnant when they come in for prenatal vitamins. You'll learn who has pneumonia. You'll learn who's using birth control. But all that information is privileged." I still remember how upset Dad was when Winston Churchill's physician wrote a book about his famous patient.

"And it's not just an autopsy," Joey was saying. "Harry Stokes's family has filed some kind of complaint with the police. I don't understand exactly what it is, but they want his death investigated."

This was something new to think about. I stored it in my mind to look at later and returned hurriedly to the pharmacy window to help a customer. Her little boy was crying loud enough to disturb everyone in the store.

Three

A few days later, Joey told me that an autopsy had been performed on Harry Stokes, but he didn't know the cause of death. Either he hadn't seen Frank since the autopsy, or his brother-in-law was no longer disseminating professional information. Most likely, it was too soon for the results to be in.

I thought about the mysteries I like to read when I can't fall asleep. Sometimes preliminary postmortem results show up quickly, but not always. It varies with the author's need to deliver red herrings before facts get in the way.

Half a dozen plots went through my mind. In a whodunit, I'd be doing some amateur detecting to catch Harry Stokes's murderer. I smiled at the thought. Which fictional sleuth would I be? I could easily identify with a V. I. Warshawski or a Kinsey Millhone. But, I thought wryly, other people would see me as Miss Marple or Jessica Fletcher. The age-old question went through my mind. Why was I, a woman who still saw herself as a thirty-five-year-old, in a fifty-five-year-old body?

With a sigh, I remembered that I couldn't be the amateur who brilliantly solved the Stokes case—not because of age, but because common sense told me Harry Stokes had probably died of a heart attack. He wasn't the first man who married a young wife and . . . Well, there were plenty of jokes along those lines. They invoked images of the fox and the sour grapes, and that was not the way I wanted to see myself.

I looked up to find Denise at the pharmacy window. She was wearing a black-and-white geometric print with a red venetian-glass necklace and matching earrings. I marveled at the way she'd found lipstick of the same red shade. In spring and fall, she wore the same dress with a flowered scarf, a deeper red, draped over one shoulder. She had *that* shade of lipstick, too.

"You looked so busy, I didn't want to interrupt," she said. "Do you have a minute to chat?"

"Actually, I was just daydreaming. But don't tell anyone or they'll say I don't need technician hours and cut Joey back."

Denise still seemed different, but I decided it was because she was quieter than usual. She must have cared more for Harry Stokes than I'd guessed. Maybe I should suggest going out together after work so she wouldn't go home to brood about might-have-beens. Mall hopping sounded like a good idea, and we could cool off at the same time.

Some of my long-time friends find it strange that Denise and I socialize outside of Food Go. "But she's a waitress," they say. "What do you talk about?" Then they focus on the differences in our education and background.

At first I explained that Denise is fun, and I need to be around someone with her lighthearted outlook. Eventually I decided I was buying into their condescending attitude when I tried to justify our friendship.

Denise and I hadn't spent much time together before Bob died, but afterward her matter-of-fact emotional support did more than all the bumblings of my other friends. Although her marriage had ended in divorce rather than death, she understood my early shock and inability to function.

She had married young and been divorced at the

age of forty. When they divided the community property, Denise got the house and her ex-husband got everything else. After twenty-two years of marriage, she found herself alone—with no skills, no children, and no relatives in Arizona. But Denise felt fortunate to get the waitress job at Food Go that my other friends scorned. And she never told me how lucky I was to have a profession.

"Will you come to the funeral with me?" Denise suddenly asked.

I hesitated. It would be awkward because I didn't really know the Stokes family other than as customers. Then I remembered what I had been thinking about. Denise was there for me when I needed her. If she had really cared about Harry Stokes and needed support at the funeral, I wouldn't let her down. I would go with her even if I had to change shifts with Tim. And that was something I usually tried to avoid.

"When is it?"

"Monday morning. Nine o'clock. At Messinger's."

At least I was off next Monday and wouldn't have to deal with Tim's reluctant consent to any kind of change. "Okay. Will you drive?"

Denise said she'd pick me up at 8:30 Monday morning. I wanted to ask about mall hopping tonight but couldn't decide if this was the right time.

"Can I come along with you to the funeral?" I hadn't realized Joey was listening to us, but he rarely missed anything that happened in the pharmacy.

Denise arranged to pick Joey up, too, and then drifted away when both phones started ringing. A doctor was on line one, returning my call. I'd phoned because his patient brought in a prescription for Prozac, an antidepressant, and the dosage seemed too high.

"Yes, doctor. I'm checking on that script for fifteen Prozac capsules. You wrote for one cap TID." I gave the Latin abbreviation for three times a day. "The recommended dosage is one QD, once daily."

"You're right, but I want to try the higher regimen

for a short time. That's why I only wrote for fifteen caps." I'd expected an argument for questioning his intentions, but he thanked me for checking it out.

"You're welcome, doctor," I said, pleased to be treated as a fellow professional.

We were so busy for the rest of the day that I was surprised when Tim, on nights this week, came in at four to begin his shift. We overlapped for an hour, not usually the most pleasant hour of my day. But today I was glad to relinquish the computer to him and concentrate on customers at the window.

A young woman, carrying a baby who looked no more than six months old, handed me a prescription for prenatal vitamins. A toddler hung onto her mother's leg with both arms. I felt sorry for the mother, but warned myself not to jump to conclusions. Maybe she wanted this third child.

When the baby started crying, I held up two lollipops, making sure only the mother could see them, and raised my eyebrows in a question.

"Wonderful!" she said as she unwrapped and delivered one to each child. "Now, Terri Sue, thank the nice lady for the sucker," she told the little girl, who released her mother's leg to grab the lollipop. Meanwhile the baby stopped crying and the mother smiled happily at me. Mother and little girl both said, "Thank you."

I gave the prescription to Joey, who took the vitamins off the shelf, handing script and bottle to Tim to generate the paperwork on the computer. Then Joey went on break so he could be back to help Tim when my shift ended.

My next customer, also with two small children in tow, had the opposite viewpoint. She was there to refill her birth control pills.

"Do you have the number?"

"Number?"

"Prescription number."

She had no idea what the number was or what kind of birth control pills she used, but I got her name and asked Tim to find her in the computer. It's easier if we have the number because then I can quickly locate the hard copy of the prescription. Otherwise we've got to sort by name on the computer. If the name is a common one or if the computer is in the process of spitting out records and labels for someone else, it takes that much longer to help the customer.

I offered lollipops, again out of the children's line of vision.

"Don't you know how bad sweets are for children?" she asked. "You ought to be ashamed of yourself."

Can't win them all, I thought, and apologized. Half an hour and five scripts later when my shift ended, I was glad to check out.

Denise was clocking out at the same time, and we walked into the Food Go parking lot together. A blast of hot, humid air contrasted sharply with the highly air-conditioned interior of the store. My relatives back east think we have a dry climate and, most of the time, they're right. But not in August.

"Any plans?" I asked Denise.

"Just to get home and collapse. We ran out of chocolate ice cream at three o'clock. And then everyone wanted chocolate and only chocolate."

I made sympathetic noises. Then I mentioned my idea about going to the mall.

"Which one?"

One thing about Scottsdale—we've got malls. Some of them are in adjoining cities and towns, but still only minutes away. Denise suggested Paradise Valley Mall, which was actually in Phoenix, but not too far from home for either of us. We agreed to meet in front of Dillards and got into our respective cars.

I took the sun shade off the windshield of my white Accord and folded it away. Then I removed the bath towel from the steering wheel and inserted the ignition key. I turned the air to its strongest setting, but the bath towel hadn't helped much. The steering wheel was so hot, I could barely force myself to get going.

Denise drives faster than I do, so I'm used to arriving last whenever we go out together. I found her right where she said she'd be, and we walked into the mall, savoring the cool air.

"Are you looking for anything special, or are we window shopping?"

"I guess I just didn't feel like going home yet," I said.

Although we both stand all day at work, walking around the mall seemed to relax us. But we still hadn't made the transition from the workday. Denise was detailing her manager's incompetence. "He knows it's hot and it will keep on being hot. And he knows chocolate is our best-selling ice cream."

Since the Food Go coffee shop only offers chocolate, vanilla, and strawberry, I could see her point. Besides, I had heard this complaint before. Denise, who worked hard to keep her customers happy, hated it when she had to disappoint them because of her manager's failures.

"You'll never believe what happened today, Ruthie. I was so angry, I finally asked why he didn't order more chocolate since we always run out. You know what that guy said?"

She didn't wait for me to guess but smiled, looking more like herself than she had since Tuesday. "He said, 'If I order more chocolate, I won't sell the other flavors.'"

We were passing a toy store when Denise grabbed my arm. "Look." She nodded toward the shop without slowing her pace. "There's Betsy Stokes."

I barely had time to wonder what a widow of three days was doing in a shopping-mall toy store, when Denise whispered, "Slow down. I want to stand here until she comes out."

"Denise, I don't think that's a good idea."

"I just want to see who the old guy is."

"What guy?"

"Don't you see the man with her?"

I glanced through the shop window. Betsy Stokes,

whom I hadn't been able to picture when we talked about her, now looked familiar. But then so did the man at her side. They were standing at a display table of windup plush animals, all in motion. The man seemed to be in perpetual motion, too, picking up each toy and inspecting it in turn.

As we watched, Betsy scooped up a toy elephant and took it to the cashier at the front of the store. When she turned, I got a better look at her. She was a tall blonde with crimped hair; even through the shop window, I could see how attractive she was. Now that I saw Betsy Stokes, I remembered that to me she always had seemed the archetypal blonde.

I hadn't filled many prescriptions for her. When she picked up Harry's various medications, my few attempts at friendly conversation had met with brief responses.

Until the moment that Betsy approached the toy-shop counter, I wasn't sure if the man was with her or just another shopper. But now I saw him hurry to her side and take out his wallet to pay for the elephant. Betsy was shaking her head and reaching in her purse, but he put his hand on her arm and smiled at her.

The smile made my pulse race, and I couldn't figure out why. "I know him," I said aloud. And then quickly, again without knowing the reason, I thought, and I like him.

Denise had pulled me over to a bench opposite the toy store, where we could seem to be in casual conversation when Betsy and her gentleman friend exited the store. "She sure likes them older," Denise muttered just as our quarry came by.

For a moment, I hoped they hadn't seen us. But Denise was determined to be noticed. "Betsy. Betsy Stokes."

Betsy turned toward us. She had green eyes that now mimed surprise. "Oh, hello Denise," she said without enthusiasm.

I remembered that they were neighbors, but maybe Betsy was embarrassed to be seen at the mall so soon after her husband's death. Denise nodded toward me and reminded Betsy that we were acquainted. "You know Ruthie Morris, from Food Go."

"Yes, of course. I'm sorry. I didn't recognize you without your white coat."

I couldn't tell if this was a put-down. Don't be so sensitive, Ruthie, I thought. People do associate you with the white-jacketed figure behind the pharmacy window. You know they rarely look at you as an individual.

It was absolutely necessary to come up with words of condolence, shopping mall or no shopping mall. I summoned up appropriate sentiments, and Betsy thanked me graciously. She was not so gracious about introducing the gentleman with her; Denise's maneuvering seemed to be in vain. However, he held out a hand to each of us, saying, "Michael Loring."

And then I knew. Was it only a few hours ago that I told myself I felt like a thirty-five-year-old? Now I was twenty again.

Michael Loring. And even without consciously recognizing him, my reaction had been the same as it was all those years ago, down in Tucson at the University of Arizona. His eyes were the same electrifying blue. As I looked into them, I thought, I should have recognized him by that overwhelming vitality, as though he were bursting with energy. He hadn't even changed so much in physical appearance. I saw some gray at the temples, but since his hair had always been light, it blended well. His face had lines that hadn't been there when we were young. They made me realize how much I'd aged, and I quickly looked away.

I wondered if I should say just two words: "Ruthie Kantor." Did I want to remind a man who was only three years older than me, a man who was with an attractive young blonde, that I was Ruth Kantor?

Two widows, I thought ironically. But what a difference. And then I was ashamed because I realized I was feeling sorry for myself, and I'd vowed never to do that again.

Denise was talking. The elephant had evidently been difficult to wrap, and its trunk stuck awkwardly out of the shopping bag. "Is that for one of Harry's grandchildren?" she asked.

"No, it's for me."

I could see Denise struggling to hide her surprise, or maybe she was trying to think of a response to Betsy's unfathomable comment. Was it possible that someone would go to the mall to buy herself a toy three days after her husband's sudden death? In my religion, the bereaved didn't even leave the house for seven days after the funeral. I had no idea what Betsy's beliefs were. But I remembered Michael Loring's religion. Oh yes, I remembered.

Denise sketched an awkward goodbye and I mumbled something, too. I couldn't concentrate on anything but my own turbulent thoughts. I hadn't seen Michael in thirty years. Closer to thirty-five years. And now he was escorting a young widow whose stepchildren believed had caused their father's death.

Four

Somehow I got through the evening of window shopping at the mall and kept up my end of the conversation when Denise and I stopped for a snack. But for once, I couldn't wait to get home and be alone with my whirling memories. During all the years that Bob and I were married, I rarely thought about Michael. He never showed up at the few class reunions I attended and, because Bob and I were happy, might-have-beens had no place in my life.

After Bob's death, I was surprised one day to find myself wondering about Michael. It happened at a low point, before I started trying to pull myself together. I was sitting at the kitchen table in a housecoat, eating a cheese sandwich that I'd thrown together. No lettuce, no tomato, no mayonnaise. I hadn't even sliced the cheese—just pulled off a chunk and stuffed it between two slices of bread. Suddenly a spasm of self-pity jolted me and I was stunned to find myself thinking, if I'd married Michael, I wouldn't be alone now. But just as this idea came into my head, I realized what I was doing to myself. I remember now, my resolve to get on with life began that day. But that determination didn't stop me from thinking occasionally of Michael.

When we first met, Michael Loring and I were both in our second year at the pharmacy school in Tucson. Only a handful of women studied pharmacy in those days, and I was asked out so often by male students, I could easily have gone to movies or college dances every night in the week. But I lived at home—most young women did in those days—and I was allowed to date only when I had no classes the next day. In our family, that meant only Saturday nights.

Fridays, when the sororities and fraternities partied, we attended synagogue services and then sat down to a sabbath dinner. My mother and father liked to invite out-of-state students to these Friday-night dinners, but they reserved this traditional hospitality for Jewish students. And Michael Loring was not Jewish.

In the 1950s, rebellion might mean wearing too much lipstick or staying out until one A.M. when your parents insisted on a midnight curfew, but for most of us, it didn't include intermarriage. When Michael and I started seeing each other, parental objections surfaced.

"We're only going to a movie," I would say. "We're friends. We're in all the same classes. We study together."

But I knew it was more than that, and I'm sure they knew it, too. Michael and I saw each other every day that semester, and we spent hours walking and talking. I had stopped dating anyone else; in the language of the Fifties, we were going steady. Unofficially.

At first I tried to keep the arguments with my parents from him. Michael called for me every Saturday night, and I was always ready to leave when he arrived at my house. I wanted to minimize the time he spent under my parents' scrutiny. They were so coldly formal, it surprised me that Michael took so long to realize something was wrong.

"Your parents don't like me," he said one evening as we left my house.

At nineteen and not very sophisticated, I didn't know what to answer. "Oh, Michael," I said and burst into tears.

"What is it? Tell me what's wrong."

Michael was only three years older than me, but he had spent two of those years in Korea. He had grown up in Boston where his dad was an attorney, and Michael also might have studied law if the army hadn't made him a medic. So I'd always considered Michael much more cosmopolitan and mature than I was.

"Tell me," he repeated.

"It's not you; they like you." I took a deep breath and blurted, "It's your religion."

"My religion! They don't even know my religion." We had gotten into his car and were riding along Speedway. "You and I have never even discussed it."

"It doesn't matter what religion. Just that you're not a Jew."

Michael quickly pulled over to the curb and turned to look at me. "I don't understand."

"Jews have very strong feelings about intermarriage," I told him. "In some traditional families, they mourn a child who marries a non-Jew as if he or she had died."

After a long silence, Michael reached over and took me in his arms. We had never talked about marriage before, and I began to be afraid that my frankness would turn him away.

"I don't think either one of us is ready to rush into marriage," he said, caressing my hair. My hair was longer then and lighter, ginger not auburn, and I wore it curled under in a pageboy style. "We both have to graduate first," he added.

"I know that."

"But I do love you, Ruthie. I tried to be patient until you were sure, but I've known my own feelings since the day I met you."

"I am sure," I said. "But it's impossible."

"It's not impossible."

My sadness was overwhelming because I'd known it would be this way. "You don't understand."

"No, I guess I don't. Your parents seem so . . . so modern."

"You mean because my father doesn't have a beard or wear a skullcap. Because mother and dad dress like anyone else."

Michael took a deep breath. "Don't link me to that kind of stereotyped thinking. You know better."

I folded my arms on the dashboard and rested my head on them. I couldn't speak. Until now, I hadn't worried about prejudices on Michael's side. I was too absorbed with those of my family.

"Look at me, Ruthie. We have to trust each other to move beyond this problem."

But even though we continued to spend time together until Michael went home that summer, we couldn't get beyond it. And in the fall, he transferred to the pharmacy college at Fordham University in New York.

I thought about Michael all weekend, between filling scripts at Food Go on Saturday and cleaning my house on Sunday. Would he be at the funeral? How did he fit into Betsy Stokes's life? And even more important, should I tell him who I was?

My mind produced a collage: the young man I'd loved in pharmacy college and the Michael I'd met in the mall Friday night, crow's feet softened at the corners of his eyes, which the harsh artificial light had revealed. I made promises to myself that I had no intention of keeping. Everything I did around the house became compulsively related to Michael: as I cleaned out the garage . . . Michael recognized me; as I dusted all the miniblinds . . . Michael walked up to me at the funeral home and said . . .

This is sick, I told myself, and five minutes later, I was throwing everything that didn't move into the washing machine and imagining another conversation—at the funeral home: Michael walked up to me and took my hand.

"Ruthie," he said in my daydream. "I recognized you the minute I saw you at the mall, but I didn't want to say anything in front of Betsy and your friend."

His eyes were as blue as I remembered them, and in my imaginings, the graying hair I had noticed at the mall was as blond as it had been years before. "I couldn't forget you," he said. "That's why I never married."

I wanted to ask him about Betsy Stokes, but that could wait because Michael was holding my hand. He smiled gently at me, "You look exactly the same as you did in pharmacy school."

The daydream reminded me of the way I felt at my twentieth birthday party, when Michael took my hand and told me he was leaving Tucson for good. That bounced me back to reality. Despite my strange state of mind since meeting Michael again, I couldn't avoid the truth of our situation. I was no longer nineteen or twenty and, romantic imaginings aside, it was nonsense to suppose Michael wouldn't know the difference. I tried to comfort myself with the undeniable fact that Michael was also thirty-five years older—but like musings of the poet Yeats, I knew the folly of being comforted. As brief as our meeting in the mall had been, I could see the same intensity behind the blue eyes and the same energy that had attracted me to Michael all those years ago. But this Michael was seeing a beautiful young blonde, a woman whose husband had just died under suspicious circumstances.

Five

When Denise picked me up on Monday, Joey was already in the car. It was obvious that all three of us had dressed carefully, toning down the bright colors of Arizona summer wear. Denise wore a turquoise and white dress with a straight skirt and large white-and-gold buttons. But her turquoise eye shadow was understated today, and her lipstick paler than usual.

"Joey was just telling me the police questioned everyone in the Stokes family," Denise said.

"That's right," Joey added. He was wearing dark gray pants with a pale gray shirt. A dark blue, discreetly patterned tie must have been borrowed for the funeral because I'd never seen it before. "My brother-in-law says they know it wasn't a heart attack."

"I hope they really zeroed in on Betsy," Denise said. "She's the one I've suspected all along. And when Ruthie and I saw her at the mall . . . Shopping, for heaven's sake. I would have been home crying my eyes out."

"People grieve in different ways," I reminded her. "That doesn't mean she drove him to suicide. And it certainly doesn't mean she murdered him."

"You never want to believe anything bad about people, Ruthie. But I've told you all along that she married him for what she could get. Harry's kids think so, too."

"How do you know?" Joey asked.

"I overheard them talking the other night. Everyone else was indoors, but Richard Stokes—that's the son—came out to smoke. His wife must have followed him outside." Denise was quiet for a few seconds while she concentrated on finding an opening for a left turn. "I guess they didn't realize I was on my patio. They were right near the fence between our yards, and I could hear every word."

Although I was curious, I couldn't bring myself to ask about the overheard conversation. But Denise didn't wait for questions. She told us Richard sounded agitated as he assured his wife the police knew something was wrong and that they suspected Betsy.

"Frank never mentioned that," Joey said.

We were pulling into the parking lot of the funeral home. "I'll tell you all the details, later," Denise promised.

Before the memorial service began, while I looked around the chapel, Denise whispered the names of the various family members to me. They were all sitting in the front row. "Richard Stokes, the son I talked about in the car. He's the first guy on the left. The one with the bald patch on top. His wife, Nancy, is next to him.. I guess they figured the grandchildren are too young to take to a funeral." She stopped and shook her head at the thought. "And Harry's daughter and her fiancé are on the other side of Nancy."

But I was no longer listening. My eyes had focused on Michael Loring sitting just past the others, next to the widow. Denise must have noticed him a moment later, for she drew in her breath and was about to speak when the memorial service began.

It doesn't make any sense, I thought. Denise accounted for all the relatives. Why is Michael sitting with the family?

The minister spoke with feeling about Harry Stokes and his contributions to the community. I gathered he'd been an active and well-respected member of his church. Although I'd liked Harry, this picture contrasted in my mind with the man who had married someone half his age and then relied on male hormones to feel young and Rogaine to fight baldness.

Perhaps I was unfair. They used to say that no man is a hero to his valet. Pharmacists may be the modern equivalents of valets. We know who's on Micronase for diabetes and who's using Anusol HC for hemorrhoids. We know who's on Antabuse to combat alcoholism and who's taking Lithium for manic depression. Like other members of the medical profession, though, we usually keep our mouths shut and our thoughts sympathetic.

The memorial service ended and all of us filed out of the chapel. We stood around the parking lot waiting for the cortege to the cemetery to form. "Look," Joey said. "There's Tim Barnard. Wasn't he supposed to be working today?"

I turned in time to see my staff pharmacist getting into his green Buick Riviera. Many of the young women who worked at Food Go seemed to be interested in Tim, though I could never understand why. Today, though, he looked particularly handsome in a dark, summer-weight suit. And for once, he had neatly brushed his thick hair back from his forehead.

Tim hadn't said a word about attending the funeral, and I was surprised to see that he cared enough about a customer to pay his respects. Out of sheer curiosity, I made a mental note to bring up the subject tomorrow at work.

Joey had drifted away, and Denise was talking to a couple of neighbors she introduced as the Brandens. They were discussing whether to go to the cemetery or to meet at the Stokeses' house afterwards.

"I don't know what's customary," Denise explained. "I'm Catholic and they're Protestants of some kind."

Raymond Branden, a short stocky man in western shirt and bolo tie, assured Denise that most people would join the mourners at the Stokeses' home after the burial. His wife explained why they weren't going to the cemetery. "I started a roast before I left this morning," Verna Branden said. "When I get home, I'll finish cooking it and take it over to their house."

Unlike the Brandens, Denise wanted to join the funeral cortege, but Joey and I talked her out of it. She agreed on condition that I visit the Stokeses with her that afternoon, and I promised, knowing I wanted to see Michael again. As we talked, I was watching him help the widow into one of the black limousines and get in beside her. I figured the chances were good that he would still be with her after the burial.

None of us said much on the way back. I had expected to hear comments from Denise, but she was quiet again, the way she had been for most of the past week.

Joey lived with his parents in one of Scottsdale's lovely condominium complexes. Denise drove past towering palms to a guarded gate and stopped. The guard peered into the car, saw Joey, and waved us through. Alternating pink and white oleander bushes, neatly trimmed, lined the driveway, leading to a huge three-tiered fountain shaped like a wedding cake but surrounded by stone coyotes. Many Scottsdale condos boast ornate fountains, but this one was a lovely sculpture. We dropped Joey off in front of the fountain.

"See you at the store later," he said, waving goodbye to both of us.

Thinking about the store made me wonder who was working in Tim's place. Maybe he had changed shifts with the relief pharmacist who worked on our days off.

"We've got a few hours to kill until we join the crowd at the Stokeses' house," Denise said. "Why don't we order a fruit basket for the family. Then we can go out for something to eat, and if it's still too early, we can wait at my house."

"I should get home and change first," I said, thinking of Michael.

She glanced at my navy print dress. "You look just right."

"It's sticking to my back. In this heat, I'll soon look like I slept in it."

"That's what you get for wearing silk when it's a hundred and seven degrees in the shade. Don't worry about the creases, Ruthie. You look great." She smiled at me. "A friend once told me creases show the integrity of the fabric; I guess she meant they tell everyone your dress isn't polyester."

"Polyester has its advantages."

I was glad that Denise seemed more like herself, and I agreed to her plans. Besides, I really did want to hear more about the conversation between Harry Stokes's son and daughter-in-law.

Denise didn't say anything about the Stokes family for a while, and I asked no questions. Now that she had emerged from her quiet spell, she appeared to go out of her way to be amusing. We chatted about work. She told me about the customer who always gave precise instructions on how he wanted everything served and then mixed it all together on his plate. I told her, without mentioning names, about one of my customers who had insisted on a description of everyone ahead of him. He intended to look for them in the store and ask them if I could fill his prescriptions first.

By the time we went to lunch at the cafeteria, we were both chatting the way we usually did. Then Denise suddenly got serious again. "I started to tell you earlier about Harry's children. His son, Richard, was going on and on about the will. He said he was pretty sure that Harry hadn't changed it."

As Denise recounted the details of the conversation she'd overheard, they seemed to substantiate what she had believed all along.

"Richard Stokes's conversation with his wife, Nancy, went like this:

"'Betsy's in for a big surprise.'

" 'You think she was surprised when Dad died?' she replied.

" 'That's not what I meant. I told you the police questioned her for hours. If there's anything to find out, they'll get it out of her.'

" 'Can we count on that? They wouldn't even have questioned her if you hadn't called with your suspicions.'

"Richard didn't respond for a moment. The only sound I could hear was the chirping of crickets on the patio. Probably puffing away, I thought, as I caught a whiff of cigarette smoke. I couldn't go back into my own house then, even if I wanted to; they would hear me.

" 'I wasn't the only one who spoke to the police,' Richard continued. 'Sheila called them, too.'

" 'Your sister? I can't believe it. I thought she was too wrapped up in her new boyfriend to notice anything else.'

" 'Listen carefully, Nancy, and try to think for once. I told the police Betsy married Dad for his money. But if he never changed his will, that takes away her motive.' He paused. 'And it gives us one.'

" 'Richard, what are you saying? No one could think *you* killed Dad.'

" 'Or you. Or Sheila. Or her new guy.'

"Nancy shrieked and her husband shushed her and said. 'Do you want everyone to hear, you fool?'

" 'You're the fool! You're the one who got the police started investigating in the first place.' Then her voice rose again.

" 'Can't you quiet down?' he hissed at her.

" 'No one can hear us. They're all inside, and the air-conditioning is blasting away.'

" 'Well, shut up and listen to me. No one knows I lost my job last month. They all think we're well off.'

" 'You can't keep it from the police,' she said.

" 'Why not? They won't check with my boss. I mean my ex-boss.'

" 'Well, what did you tell them?'

"'They asked me my occupation. I told them I'm an aerospace engineer.' Now his voice got louder. 'Damn it, I am one even though I was laid off.'

"Again there was silence for a while. I couldn't see into their yard because the block fence is too high, but I imagined Richard was puffing on his cigarette and thinking. Then I heard 'Richard, what are we going to do?'

"'Nothing.'

"'But what if they question us again?'

"'We've got nothing to hide. After all, if Dad hadn't remarried, there'd be no question about the money.'

"Then Nancy murmured something that I didn't catch. But I heard Richard's answer: 'No, we don't have to wait long. I explained it all to you before. Dad had everything in a living trust, so there's no probate. We'll get the money very soon.'

"They went indoors then and, after a few minutes, I returned to my house. I couldn't sleep well that night because the conversation I overheard kept running through my mind.

"What do you make of it?" she asked me now.

"I don't know, but I think we'd better leave it to the Scottsdale Police Department."

"Well, I don't have much confidence in the police. After all, they never questioned me."

I thought Denise was carrying things too far. "Why should they question you?"

"You know I wanted Harry for myself. The truth is I hate Betsy for taking him away from me."

If Denise's aim was to startle me, she had succeeded. I decided laughter was the best reaction. "Denise, in that case, you would have killed Betsy. And, as far as I could see this morning, she's still very much alive."

"It may sound funny to you, but maybe I brooded all these months about being scorned."

I took a different tack. "Why do you want to be a suspect? We don't even know yet if Harry was murdered?"

"*She* murdered him, but I don't mind being a suspect. Not if it leads to an investigation. I just don't want them to say suicide and close the case."

I had no answer to that and changed the subject. We picked up the fruit basket we'd ordered before lunch and drove to Denise's house. Although I had been there before, I had never seen her neighborhood in the daytime. She pointed out the Stokes house next to hers on the east and the Branden house on the west. I'd wondered why someone as wealthy as Harry Stokes was reputed to be would live next door to Denise. Even though she and her ex-husband had been comfortable, they certainly had not been rich. But when I saw the Stokes house, I understood.

It was on a corner lot, at one end of a cul-de-sac, and it was much larger than the other homes on the same street. From its Spanish-tile roof to the freshly painted block exterior, the house, with its spacious, well-kept grounds, looked luxurious.

"That was the original house on the property," Denise explained. "Years ago, the owners sold off the rest of the land for development. But they kept the house and about a half acre for themselves."

Denise pulled into her carport and led the way into her own house. "Harry and his first wife were only the second owners. Of course, they did a lot of remodeling."

"Did you know the first wife?" I asked.

"No, she died before we moved in, at least nine or ten years ago. That's why everyone was so surprised when he suddenly married again. After all this time, we thought he wasn't interested in remarriage."

We were sitting in Denise's kitchen, overlooking her patio and pool. The pool was kidney-shaped, a very popular type in Scottsdale. My own pool was a rectangular one, designed for swimming laps in a relatively small area.

From the air, the swimming pools look like little turquoise jewels. Tourists always comment about them when they fly into Sky Harbor Airport for the first time. But when they land and confront the desert heat, people begin to realize why backyard pools aren't considered luxuries here.

"But Denise," I said. "Even if Harry's remarriage surprised you, nothing you've said so far means that Betsy drove him to suicide or killed him."

She suddenly got up and loomed over my chair. "Well, I live right next to them, and if I told you everything I saw and heard over the last few months, you'd believe me."

Six

When we walked next door to the Stokes house, I was surprised at the striking black-and-white decor of its contemporary interior, which contrasted sharply with the southwestern exterior. A buffet lunch was set up in the formal dining room, and people walked about with plates of food in their hands. The crowd was large enough to spill over into the living and family rooms.

"Too bad it's so hot outside; their patio is beautiful," Denise whispered. "And be sure to notice the kitchen. They just spent thirty thousand dollars remodeling it."

I was too busy scanning the crowd for Michael Loring to care about the patio or the kitchen. Richard Stokes was talking to some people in one corner of the living room. His back was toward me, but I knew him by the distinctive bald patch. Unlike his late father, the son didn't seem to be using Rogaine to grow hair again. Maybe his wife liked the bald spot; some women did.

For the first time, I got a clear view of Nancy Stokes—I recognized her by the mauve dress she'd been wearing at the memorial service. Although she couldn't have been much older than Betsy, her stepmother-in-law, her short brown hair was starting to gray. She was a thin, tired-looking woman, in sharp contrast to Betsy, who had seemed bursting with vitality when we saw her at the mall.

Harry's daughter, Sheila, had changed to white tennis shorts and a T-shirt that said SCOTTY'S GROUPIE in large purple letters. I knew her by her long French braid and reflected how different all of them had looked from where I sat, eight rows back, in the chapel. The only people I could be sure to recognize were Betsy Stokes and Michael Loring, and when Denise pulled me along to the newly remodeled kitchen, I finally saw them.

The kitchen, starkly sophisticated with its black laminate counters and stainless-steel built-ins, wasn't too crowded. They were sitting at the table, a huge granite slab, and Michael seemed to be talking earnestly to Betsy. She nodded her head occasionally but, whenever people approached the table, stopped the conversation to speak to them. I guessed some of the earliest visitors were taking leave of her, reiterating their condolences, while she was thanking them for coming.

Although I'd made up my mind to talk to Michael today, I found I couldn't interrupt. Ruthie, you know that's just an excuse, I told myself, but I left the kitchen without a word to anyone.

Denise seemed restless but remained at my side, and I knew I didn't want to speak to Michael until she was busy elsewhere. As we stood at the buffet table, helping ourselves to fruit salad, Mrs. Branden came over to point out her roast to Denise. I drifted back to the kitchen.

I leaned against the silver-and-black refrigerator, holding my paper plate and pretending to eat, while I waited for someone to distract Betsy so I could talk to Michael alone. In my mind, I worked out ways to reveal my identity. Maybe the subtle approach would be best. "Do you ever reminisce about pharmacy school?" or "I haven't seen you at our reunions." No, that was too coy; I would be direct. "Do you remember me, Michael? I'm Ruthie Kantor Morris."

After a while, a young couple came over to talk to Betsy, and I quickly went to Michael's side of the kitchen table. He had stood politely at the couple's approach and now turned his full attention, along with that forceful blue gaze, to me. I hesitated.

"We met at the mall the other night," I began.

"Yes," he said. "I see you no longer spend Friday nights at the synagogue."

I couldn't hide my surprise. "You recognized me."

"Not right away," he admitted. "But before you and your friend walked away, I knew."

"You didn't say anything."

"I didn't want to upset Betsy. She has enough on her mind."

I was silent. He took my arm and led me from the kitchen to a quiet corner of the formal dining room, opposite the laden buffet table. My mind was racing, but I could only think in clichés. "Well, it's certainly been a long time" or "How strange to meet this way." A saying of my mother's, "We should meet at a happy occasion next time," nearly made me giggle, and I realized I could easily make a fool of myself if I didn't control my nervousness.

Michael was still staring at me, but I couldn't read his expression. I wanted to ask how he'd recognized me, but I didn't dare. He surprised me again.

"You were sporting your serious look. That time just before your birthday, you looked at me exactly the same way."

I remembered every detail of that afternoon because I'd relived it hundreds of times. And I felt the same pain now that had overwhelmed me so many years ago.

It was close to the end of our second year of pharmacy school. I didn't know yet that Michael had applied for a transfer to a pharmacy college in New York.

Arizona weather in May can be pretty hot even in Tucson, although Tucson, with its higher elevation, is slightly cooler than Scottsdale. That day, the day

Michael and I knew we'd soon part, was comfortably breezy, and we were walking on campus between classes. The scene between us could have come from one of my favorite books of those days, *Marjorie Morningstar* by Herman Wouk.

Michael led me to a shady spot under a grapefruit tree. "Let's touch down here," he said. Even his choice of verbs reflected his boundless energy. Michael never told people he intended to go somewhere; he would just dash upstairs or rush over. That crackling vitality had first attracted me. It never moderated, even in the Arizona heat.

I leaned against the tree and watched Michael. He seemed unusually quiet.

"We need to talk about our future," he said.

"Why can't we stay as we are?"

"Because I don't want to run home for the summer and leave you here."

I looked up at the tree. The season was over; most of the fruit had been picked or fallen to the ground months ago, but a few grapefruit clung tenaciously to the highest branches. "There's nothing we can do."

"Damn it! There are plenty of choices, Ruthie. But you have to be willing to make some hard decisions."

"You know we're both still in school."

"I've figured it out. I can get close to full-time work on nights and weekends during the school year. If you're willing to work part-time, we can afford to get married."

Married to Michael. How I wanted to shout, "Yes, let's forget everything else and do it." But although I'd be twenty years old in a few weeks, girls brought up in traditional middle-class homes didn't give up their families so easily in those days. We were less sophisticated than today's young women; even the fact that we were called "girls" then, and lived at home until marriage, underlines how different the times were.

Now, in Betsy Stokes's dining room, Michael gently touched my shoulder. "You're thinking about those two kids under the grapefruit tree in Tucson."

"Yes," I admitted and turned away from his intense gaze.

"How have the years been for you, Ruthie? I know you're married because your name is different."

I couldn't bring myself to tell him about Bob. If I say that I'm a widow, I thought, somehow it will sound all wrong. And what about Betsy? I can't compete with her, even if I want to. Later, when I got away from the force of Michael's personality, I would have to look closely at that last thought.

Michael must have noticed my reluctance to answer, for he started to tell me about himself. He had married right after graduation from Fordham, but the marriage had not lasted long. He changed to a less personal topic.

"Are you a practicing pharmacist? Where do you work?"

That was an easier subject for me. I told him about Food Go, and we discussed the changes in pharmacy over the years. We laughed about the ointments and suppositories we'd learned to compound in school and how unlikely it would have seemed then to dispense only prepackaged medications.

"Remember when we were supposed to make peppermint water in the lab and ran out of time?"

My awkwardness and unease vanished for the moment and I smiled warmly at him, delighting in the memory. "You were the one who decided to dissolve a peppermint Lifesaver in the mixture."

"Well, the professor thought it was the best peppermint water he'd ever tasted." Michael's lips curved upward and his eyes caught fire the way I remembered, the way they once made me want to be with him forever. But forever had been only one academic year.

It was odd that I'd just been thinking about *Marjorie Morningstar,* because the fictional Marjorie and what she represented had influenced my breakup with Michael. The family in the novel was like mine, even though we lived so far from Marjorie's New York

City. And when she rejected her first love and later became engaged to someone else, I agonized with Marjorie as she confessed the early affair to her fiancé. Her guilt was overwhelming because in those days "good Jewish girls" were expected to be virgins when they married.

The part of Herman Wouk's novel that had affected me most was the reaction of Marjorie's husband-to-be to her confession; he never again mentioned the subject, but he never again wore the same joyful look. The double standard was very real in the 1950s, and I knew I was not going to disappoint my husband like Marjorie Morningstar. That's why, after I turned down Michael's marriage proposal, I also turned down his plea to go east with him anyhow.

Michael must have noticed that I'd stopped laughing and was looking serious again, but I didn't want him to know which tape my mind was running on its multimedia screen. He, too, became serious.

"Ruthie, were you Harry Stokes's pharmacist?"

"Yes."

"I must talk to you. There are too many unresolved questions about his death, and I need to know what prescription drugs he was taking."

"Don't the police . . ." I started to ask. As I spoke, I could see Betsy crossing the room toward us. Michael was watching her, too.

"They seem to suspect Betsy," he said quickly. His voice caught and he cleared his throat to cover it. "I have to help her."

Seven

Seeing your first love after thirty-five years should be comic, I thought, not traumatic. After all, even when the years are kind, how can any of us live up to the memories and retouched photos in our minds? But again, I identified with the poet Yeats, who knew the folly of being comforted. And I, too, wasn't finding it easy to be wise, because the years had only intensified the impact of Michael's vibrant personality.

I reminded myself I knew nothing about this Michael or the kind of person he was now. What was his relationship to Betsy and why was he so concerned about her? And most of all, if Michael walked into Food Go, would I tell him what he wanted to know? I resolved to look at the patient profile for Harry Stokes the first thing next morning, so that I'd know what prescription drugs he was getting before Michael asked for the information.

I had no opportunity to call up the record on the computer. Food Go, like most supermarket chains out here, is open twenty-four hours a day, although the pharmacy has shorter hours. When I got there on Tuesday morning, Michael was waiting for me. He was inside the store, pacing in front of the pharmacy window.

"I didn't know your schedule, so I thought I'd just come in." He looked toward the coffee shop. "I'll jump out of the way while you open up. See you in a few minutes."

I unlocked the door, flipped on the lights, stepped onto the raised floor of the pharmacy, and started my opening procedure. Nowadays, we depend on the computer just like other businesses do. I turned the monitor on and keyed in my password. Then, I quickly initialized today's disk and was ready to begin.

The main office had relayed two messages overnight, and I printed them. One warned about someone forging Rx's for Vicodin, a painkiller with hydrocodone. The forger had a clever modus operandus—he first asked for a generic drug to allay suspicion and then for Vicodin. I smiled at the description—between 5 feet, 7 inches and 6 feet, 1 inch with either light hair or dark hair—and wondered how we were supposed to recognize him.

The other message reminded us that inventory was scheduled in three weeks and asked that we cut down our orders as much as possible. I put both messages on the small bulletin board for Tim and Joey to see and looked up to find Michael watching me through the glass windows. When I slid them open, he handed me a cup of coffee and a pastry from the coffee shop.

"I hope you haven't lost your craving for cheese danish," he said.

"No, but they still call them breakfast rolls out here."

"So they do." Michael leaned over the counter and put his own coffee cup down.

"Share?" I asked, moving the pastry back toward him. Then I wanted to pull the word in because it brought the past reeling back.

"Share," Michael agreed and grinned so warmly at me that I had to grip my side of the counter for support.

Any minute now the phone will ring or customers will come to the window and rescue me, I thought. You can hold on long enough, Ruthie. Don't be a fool.

"Does it sound odd to say the last few days have had some of the saddest and happiest moments," Michael said. "When I woke up Friday morning, I never dreamed we'd meet again before the day was over."

"It was a shock for me, too." I had meant to say "surprise," but the word "shock" escaped before I realized it.

"We didn't get to talk much yesterday. Do you have to be home right away or can we meet after you finish here?"

"Five o'clock," I said and excused myself to help a customer at the window.

Unlike some of my friends who hang around and talk while I try to work, Michael quickly stood aside and waited for me to be free again. When I was, he returned to the window.

"Ruthie, I need to know what prescription drugs Harry Stokes was taking."

I hedged. "You know I haven't had a chance to look up his record."

"Could you do it now?"

"Why?"

Michael sounded impatient. "It's important. I told you all about it yesterday."

It was my turn to be brusque. "You didn't tell me anything, Michael. Anything that would justify my breaching patient confidentiality."

"Patient confidentiality! The patient is dead."

"As far as I'm concerned, that doesn't make any difference," I flared. "Haven't you ever done any continuing education in pharmacy ethics?"

Michael's eyes flickered, but I could see he was trying hard to control himself. "This is not idle curiosity. I need to know what Harry was taking."

"After you talked to me yesterday, I thought about it all evening. I don't see how I can give you that information. But I'll be glad to give it to the police."

"The police," Michael exploded. "All they want to do is railroad Betsy. They can't believe that a young woman could marry an older man for anything but his money."

"I'm sure *you* want to believe it was love," I said and then was ashamed at my sarcastic tone.

"What's that supposed to mean?"

"Just what I said."

He stared at me for a few seconds. "You certainly have changed," he said and walked away. I could see the doors leading into the parking lot from the pharmacy window and, after a moment, Michael's tall figure hurrying out of the store.

My face felt flushed, and I was so shaken that I had to sit down. I couldn't believe Michael and I, meeting again after so many years, had quarreled. It's a matter of principle this time, too, I insisted aloud, but there was no one to hear. I asked myself whether I was being self-righteous to mask jealousy. If Michael hadn't been spending his time with the young widow, would I have given him the prescription printout? I didn't know the answer.

From time to time during that long day, I had to choke back tears. My identity as a professional helped as it had during Bob's long illness and death. I was here for people who needed their medication, not to indulge in self-pity. So I concentrated on filling prescription after prescription.

When Joey came in at ten o'clock, he looked solemn as he told me his brother-in-law was going out to the Stokes house again to talk to Betsy.

"Why?"

"I only know what Frank said. They have some questions for her."

Maybe Betsy did drive her husband to suicide, I thought. After all, she had Michael waiting in the wings. I wanted to ask whether the police thought it was suicide or murder, but that seemed too melodramatic. Anyhow, it wasn't right to pump Joey when he shouldn't have had the information in the first place.

The day dragged along. Even Joey was quieter than usual, as though he'd sensed my mood, and for once I was looking forward to Tim's arrival. One hour after he comes in, I'll be able to go home, I thought. Then I can let go. But I found I no longer wanted to cry; I wanted only to search my heart and see what meeting Michael again really meant to me.

A few times, Joey started to talk to me and seemed to change his mind. I really must lighten up, I thought. It's not fair to him to make his workday miserable, too.

"Joey, I know I've been a bear today, but it's not anything you did. You don't have to tiptoe around me."

"It's not that," he said. "I need some advice, but I didn't want to bother you."

The telephone rang before I could reassure him. Simultaneously, two customers appeared at the window, and I went to help them while Joey grabbed the phone. As soon as we're both free again, I promised myself, I'll find out what's on his mind.

Just before four o'clock, we had some breathing space. Joey left the computer and walked over to the counter where I was working on the reorder list. Usually when he wanted advice, it was about his plans to go to medical school. I waited, noticing how drawn the young face looked. I saw shadows under the dark eyes and blamed myself for not talking him out of summer courses at ASU. It was hard enough to work and go to school full-time during the rest of the year.

"About two weeks ago," Joey began, but was interrupted by Tim, who walked into the pharmacy and muttered a hello to me. For Joey, his only greeting was a raised eyebrow and nod toward the ringing phone, uncalled for because Joey already had his hand on the receiver.

"For Mrs. McCullough? Her hydrochlor . . . what? Do you mean HCTZ?"

I listened approvingly while I did some paperwork that was due before I could leave for the day. Joey was a good technician, and I could trust him to handle refills.

"What strength, twenty-five milligrams or fifty? Did she give you the prescription number? That's okay; we'll find it." Joey hung up the phone and said, "I hope the original really was filled at this store." He started toward the computer to look it up, but Tim pushed him away.

"I'll take care of it. You go and unpack the order."

I suppose I should have put a stop long ago to Tim bullying our technicians, but Joey and I both try to ignore it rather than turn the place into a battlefield. Luckily, Joey doesn't seem to hold a grudge; any other technician would have quit after one week.

"Saw you at the funeral," he said to Tim. "We didn't know you were going to be there."

"I knew the family in Tucson."

Before I had a chance to ask Tim about that, two people appeared at the window to pick up their prescriptions, and both phones began to ring. We were too rushed for conversation during the next hour, and my shift ended before I had time to clock watch. In fact, we were so busy that I clocked out twenty minutes late.

I walked into the parking lot, relieved that my workday was over, and I no longer had to put up a professional front to hide my personal turmoil. Now I could relax and consider what to do about Michael. In immediate contradiction to this thought, I saw him approach from the tree-shaded part of the lot. As Michael walked toward me, the sunlight accentuated the blond strands in his graying hair and, from the distance, he looked exactly the way I remembered him. "Your well-belovèd's hair has threads of grey," as a friend had told Yeats. When I saw Michael approach that afternoon, I realized how sorry I was that I'd sent him away again. I knew once more that time had not made me any wiser than the poet.

I didn't move until Michael reached me. Even though I was still up on the sidewalk and he was in the parking lot, he was a head taller than me. Michael took my hand, and the gesture was so natural that I stepped down and followed him without a word. He unlocked the door on the passenger side of his car, a silver-and-gray Lexus, and held it open for me, then went around and took down the sun shield. It must have been 140 degrees in the parked car, so I kept my door open until he started the air conditioning.

"I found an interesting Mexican restaurant not too far from here. Is that all right with you?"

In Scottsdale it's easy to find any kind of restaurant you want, so I was curious to see his choice. We pulled in front of Marilyn's First Mexican Restaurant, a place I'd never tried. Michael always had a knack for discovering restaurants with good food, even when we were students with limited funds. But I wondered whether he'd lost his touch. This place was too pretty; it seemed like part of the tourist scene rather than a restaurant serving authenic Mexican food.

We went through the brick patio with its chairs and tables covered in bright primary colors. As we waited to be seated, I watched a young woman in Mexican dress rolling out tortillas at a counter just inside the entryway.

The restaurant, with its high-backed booths upholstered in blue and its red and yellow seats, had a relaxed atmosphere. When we were seated and had ordered our beverages, Michael smiled at me. "How little you've changed."

And how different that statement was from his angry words in the pharmacy. "I was thinking the same about you," I said aloud. My reading glasses were on now as I scanned the menu. "Maybe that's why nature dims our sight as we grow older."

"You know, Ruthie, I've thought about the past all day today. And I made up my mind that I wasn't going to give up so easily this time."

I didn't know if he meant our relationship or his demand for Harry Stokes's prescription record. The waiter approached, so I could avoid a reply while we scanned the menus. Like many Arizona restaurants during the off-season, Marilyn's offered a "sunset menu" with considerable savings. I was careful to choose spinchada from the specials, but Michael ordered beef chimichangas, which were on the regular menu. Spinchada was a dish I'd never heard of, but it was vegetarian and the description intrigued me. A spinach enchilada in a white sauce, topped with almond slivers.

"I blame myself for not fighting for you," Michael said as soon as the waiter walked away.

Had he been that unhappy? My own misery was overwhelming at first, but when I met Bob Morris about two years later, I was ready to fall in love again. Once in a while, I wondered about Michael, but Bob and I were happy and those thoughts were fleeting.

Now I looked across the table at Michael. Despite the heat, he was wearing a white shirt with thin burgundy stripes, a burgundy tie with a navy-and-white pattern, and navy slacks. I couldn't remember if he'd been dressed more casually that morning, so I didn't know whether he'd changed for dinner with me.

My own gold-and-white print dress, polyester and cotton today, was a compromise between the demands of my long workday and the expectation of seeing Michael again. I searched my mind for a more comfortable topic than our breakup and realized we hadn't yet talked about our lives since pharmacy college. He must have been thinking along the same lines.

"Tell me about yourself, Ruthie. All I know is that you're Mrs. Morris now."

I took a deep breath and told him about Bob, not my first love—but my love just the same. I didn't say that, of course. When I got to Bob's death, he reached across the table and lightly touched my hand for a moment. The shock of his touch was so intense, I dropped my eyes like a nineteenth-century heroine to hide my reaction. But I think he felt it, anyhow.

"There's something I want you to know," he said.

"I'm not wining and dining you to get the Rx printout."

I pointed to my iced tea. "Hardly wining."

The waiter brought our tortilla chips and salsa. By the time we'd each helped ourselves, I'd decided how to ask the main question on my mind. "Why are you so anxious to help Betsy?"

"I thought I should be here for her for as long as she needs me," Michael said.

His words struck with such force, I had to work to keep my teeth unclenched. I felt like chewing my nails, something I hadn't done since childhood. More than that, I wanted to rage at the unfairness of it when we had just met again after so many years apart. Luckily, Michael didn't seem to expect a reply because I had none to give.

"She has no one else," he continued.

"What about her stepchildren?"

"Unfortunately they haven't tried to know Betsy as a person. She needs friends now, but they haven't given her a chance." Michael's voice rose slightly. "She's too decent to complain, but I know how badly they've treated her."

I bit my lips, willing myself to silence.

"That's why I'm trying to spend as much time as possible with her," he said. He was holding a tortilla chip in midair, obviously too agitated to eat it.

He certainly can rationalize, I thought cynically. It's not her long blond hair or her green eyes; he's just helping her out.

"You see," Michael continued, "her mother remarried and moved to London after our divorce. I'm the only one she has now."

"Oh," I said, drawing out each word, ashamed of my thoughts but relieved at the same time. "Betsy is your—your daughter."

"That's why I want the police to stop bothering her. I know they always suspect the spouse when they can't explain a death, so I've got to unearth what really happened. Before it's too late," he added.

"But how will the prescription record accomplish that? What was the cause of Harry's death?"

"He went into a diabetic coma and his heart failed."

"That shouldn't have happened. His diabetes was under control."

Michael put the chip down uneaten and added more salsa to it. "I'm convinced he took something that caused a reaction. But what could have interacted with his other prescriptions?"

"How can you be sure it was a fatal interaction?"

"Listen, Ruthie, we *know* he didn't commit suicide. He and Betsy were happy. Very happy," he emphasized.

He didn't meet my eyes when he said that, and I wondered briefly about his insistence. Was he holding something back?

"If Harry was taking two drugs that were contraindicated, we would have known it when we filled the second script. Didn't you find the vials?"

"We found Micronase, Lopressor, Oreton, and Rogaine."

I ran them over in my mind. Micronase for his diabetes and Lopressor to control his blood pressure. I remembered he'd been on those for quite a while. He'd been taking Oreton, the male hormone, since his marriage. The same was true of Rogaine to grow back hair. No interactions there at all. "Maybe he had something filled elsewhere," I said.

The waiter materialized with two large platters. One taste of spinchada and that was the end of my reverse snobbery about upscale Mexican restaurants. This was gourmet cooking, which didn't stop me from pouring the rest of the salsa over everything on the plate.

"It's possible, of course, that he went to more than one doctor and more than one pharmacy, but we haven't found anything else except OTCs."

I doubted whether anyone could commit suicide

with over-the-counter drugs, but even aspirins can be fatal if you take enough of them. We were both silent for a while as we worked at our dinners, but it was a comfortable silence this time.

"I'm sorry about the way I behaved this morning, Ruthie. I don't want you to compromise your ideals."

A quick glance at Michael's face showed me that he was not being sarcastic. "And I'm sorry I lost my temper," I said.

"No, you were right. I realize now you didn't even know Betsy is my daughter."

I hoped we weren't going back to the sticky topic of patient confidentiality. Was a father-in-law entitled to the records of his deceased son-in-law? And how much privacy was left to Harry Stokes? His wife and Michael now knew what he may have carefully hidden from them: he was using Rogaine to suppress baldness and Oreton to restore potency. I was sure from what I had seen of Harry and his careful grooming that he would have guarded this information while he was alive. On the other hand, I doubted that he could have concealed his diabetes and high blood pressure.

"Here's what I've been thinking," Michael continued. "I won't ask you to give me a printout since you consider that unethical. But could you scan the record and tell me whether you see anything that we didn't find, anything that would interact fatally." He stopped me before I could speak. "Don't answer now. Think it over and I'll be in the store tomorrow afternoon."

We talked about Michael's job; he was the pharmacy director at one of the Tucson hospitals. We talked about the differences between Tucson and Scottsdale. We talked about everything except whether we were going to pick up where we had left off so many years ago. But the conversation flowed as if we had known each other forever, and in a way we had.

Just before we finished our dinners, Michael asked how I liked my spinchada. He seemed hesitant, and I couldn't understand why. After a pause, he went on, "I was wondering if you ordered a vegetarian meal because you still observe the dietary laws?"

I remembered how curious he'd always been about Jewish traditions. "Bob's family weren't observant Jews," I explained, "so I gradually became less religious after we were married."

Michael looked surprised. "I thought it meant so much to you."

"It did. I suppose if we'd had children, I would have continued my own family's ways."

"Only for your children, not for yourself?" His eyes held mine. "It's rather ironic, Ruthie. I would have encouraged you to keep your traditions."

Eight

I was on the day shift again on Wednesday, and I arrived at Food Go early, resolved to look up Harry Stokes's prescription file right away. Although our pharmacy doesn't open until nine in the morning, customers often show up as soon as I turn on the lights. So this time I went through my opening routine in the dark to avoid interruptions. Then I typed in Stokes, Harry and looked at his prescription history. At first, I found just what I expected to see. On July 29, only four days before his death, he had renewed his Rogaine and Oreton prescriptions.

The previous entry showed Micronase, 5 milligrams, which I hadn't remembered at that dosage. Well, no wonder; Tim had filled it. Up until June, Harry was getting 2½ milligrams, but in July, his doctor had increased the dosage. It looked like Harry hadn't been controlling his diet and exercise. His doctor had also increased the Lopressor, and the higher strength indicated Harry's blood pressure must have been climbing.

I sat there in the dark and thought about what the little screen showed. Was Harry worried that his health was deteriorating? Was depression a possible side effect of his medications? I would have to read the package inserts and remind myself about any side effects.

But then I got up and looked at those white letters

on my blue computer screen again. Would a man who was depressed and about to commit suicide care about growing more hair? He had refilled his Rogaine prescription only a few days before his death. It didn't make sense to me, but it wasn't enough to build theories on.

I looked up at the clock and saw I still had twenty minutes before opening, so I thought about Michael. Should I discuss the record with him? He already knew about all four prescriptions, and he must surely have seen the fill dates on the vials. But did he know about the increased dosages, and had he considered the psychological implications?

Someone was rapping on the pharmacy window. I looked at the clock again; it was still too early to open, but I told myself the customer is always right and stepped over to the light switch.

This customer was wrong. He wanted his wife's Premarin refilled, and he wanted it now. "I have to get your doctor's okay," I told him. "But he doesn't take calls before nine."

"You're the only one who has to call the doctor," he told me. "The other lady never bothers me."

"The other lady?"

"Yes. She just fills it and doesn't give me all this crap."

"Sir, I'm the only woman at this pharmacy."

"Don't tell me that. I want my wife's medicine."

"Sir, I'll try to reach your doctor and have it for you as soon as possible." I suppressed a sigh, hoping this encounter didn't presage a difficult day. "Do you have some shopping to do elsewhere in the store?" I asked him. "Why don't you try us again at about nine fifteen?" I turned away and picked up the phone before he could say anything else, but I could hear him just the same.

"Damn lady druggists," he muttered.

Can't win, I thought, and held the phone through a recorded message that told me the doctor's office would open at 9:30.

When Joey arrived two hours later, I had filled about a dozen prescriptions and had five more lined up on the counter, waiting for him to run them through the computer, print the labels, and stack them with the scripts ready for me to fill. He was shouting to me as he came through the door to the pharmacy.

"They arrested her!"

"Oh, no," I said. "Not Betsy Stokes." Poor Michael, I thought.

"Not her. Denise."

"What?" Now I was the one to raise my voice. "How could Denise have anything to do with Harry Stokes's death?"

"I don't know the details," Joey said. "But Frank told my sister, and she called me just before I left for work."

I sat down, my mind racing. Denise lived next door to the Stokeses, and I knew she'd been infatuated with Harry. I certainly had heard enough diatribes against Betsy after the marriage. But murder? . . . I thought about Denise and how she had looked and acted since Harry's death. Subdued, yes, but that seemed natural enough in light of her infatuation. Denise had not been acting like someone with murder on her conscience; in any case, I was convinced she couldn't commit murder.

The stock comment of parents, friends, and acquaintances everywhere: I don't believe it. She was kind, quiet, a good person—you name it. And yet, I really couldn't believe it.

I remembered our conversation after the funeral when Denise seemed to be complaining because the Scottsdale police hadn't questioned her. She'd admitted hating Betsy, but what did that have to do with Harry's death?

For the rest of the day, I tried to concentrate on doing my job without making mistakes. I triple-checked each prescription because I knew I wasn't thinking clearly.

Michael had said he'd be in that afternoon, but he

hadn't shown by the time Tim arrived to relieve me. We had no overlap today, so I didn't wait; I removed my white jacket, hung it neatly on a coat hook, clocked out, and walked over to the coffee shop.

As I did, I tried to remember Denise's schedule for this week, but hers was more confusing than mine. Then I mentally formed questions for the other waitress to extract information without giving anything away.

Even before I reached the coffee shop, I could see a chubby young woman resetting one of the tables. What was her name again? Ellen, and she didn't want to be called Ellie.

"Ellen, has Denise left for the day?"

"Left? She hasn't even been in. They called me early this morning." Her round face took on an aggrieved look. "I wasn't supposed to be here until four, but I had to get the kids to the sitter and rush over here."

"Is she sick?" I asked cautiously.

"What do I know? My manager told me it was an emergency, and I'd better get to the store right away. So I did."

I tried to sound casual. "Oh, well. I'll catch her tomorrow."

Ellen was still talking as I walked away. "Didn't even say please. Just wanted me to drop everything and work two shifts."

All the way home, I wondered whether to call Denise. Ordinarily I wouldn't have hesitated. I'd phone to see how she was feeling and whether she needed anything. But after Joey's news, maybe it would be better to reach Michael and see what he had heard. No, he might think I was looking for an excuse to call him, and I didn't want that.

I arrived home without reaching a decision. Kicking off my shoes, I turned the air down to 70 degrees and went into the family room to check my answering machine. The light was blinking, and the digital readout showed three messages. After pitches from two salesmen, evidently not deterred by the machine, I heard Denise's voice.

"Ruthie, I know you'll be tired and hungry when you hear this, but I need to see you. Please come right over."

I was so relieved to realize Denise must be at home that I put on my shoes and rushed out the door. It didn't take long to reach her house. Despite my concern for her, though, I couldn't help wondering about Michael again as I passed the Stokes's place and saw his Lexus in the driveway. I pulled into Denise's carport.

Denise answered the door within seconds after the chimes sounded. She was wearing a T-shirt, white shorts, and running shoes—the summer uniform in Arizona, except on the job. It's also the winter uniform, but only for tourists. Her long hair, usually so carefully curled and brushed, looked uncombed. No eye shadow today and no earrings. Her eyes were red, but I couldn't tell whether it was from fatigue or from tears.

"Thank God you're here," she said. "I didn't know who to turn to."

She led me from the small Mexican-tiled entryway into her living room. Denise's furniture, unlike Betsy's, brought the southwestern style of the house indoors. I sat down on her sofa, trying to make myself comfortable against a trio of throw pillows with sandpainting motifs.

"What happened?" I thought it better not to repeat Joey's story that she'd been arrested.

"The police were here at seven this morning. I was getting ready for work and they waited while I finished dressing. Then I had to call Food Go to say I wouldn't be in." Denise stopped and her face reflected the surprise she must have felt. "They wanted to question me." She sounded indignant rather than upset.

My role should have been to dispense sympathy, but I was so relieved to hear she hadn't been arrested that I blurted, "Well, only the other day you complained because they hadn't questioned you."

"People say a lot of things when they're upset."

"Yes, I know."

"They started questioning me, and they sounded like they thought I killed Harry. So, before I realized what I was saying, I told them they were wrong. That I loved Harry."

Uh-oh, I thought.

"Then the questioning got worse. Hell hath no fury and all that."

"It got worse?"

"They asked me how long Harry and I had been sleeping together."

I gripped the carved wooden arms of the sofa in shock. Could they be right? Then I was angry at myself for doubting Denise. My expression must have revealed that first reaction.

"It's not true," she said. Her voice was stiff.

"I know."

"But you wondered if there was fire along with the smoke. Ruthie, if you doubt me, what chance do I have with everyone else?"

She was right, and the knowledge made me uncomfortable. We were friends; but for a brief moment, I'd thought the police must have evidence of an affair. How odd that Joey's news didn't make me believe she could commit murder, but this had nearly changed my mind.

"Fantasies are one thing," Denise said. "You know about them. I used to talk to you because you were so sympathetic."

"Yes, I remember." I also remembered my own daydreams about Harry and was glad I'd never mentioned them. Suddenly I had a terrible fear that the police would suspect me of an affair with Harry. Would they believe my denials any more than Denise's? I could feel the throw pillows digging into my back and reached behind to adjust them.

"They questioned me for hours," she said. "I could

have called a lawyer, but I know I haven't done anything wrong. I work too hard to throw money away on a lawyer."

"I still don't understand why they suspect you."

"Could be someone told the police I hang around the pharmacy a lot. They think I had access to something."

"What?" I was outraged now. Yet an inner voice reminded me that I could be suspected for the same flimsy reasons that had momentarily made me doubt Denise.

"They wouldn't even tell me what drug. I said I've never gotten anything from you without a prescription."

"Of course not. They must know I can't just hand out drugs to my friends."

Denise looked away as if to gather her courage. She was sitting next to me on the sofa and had thrown one of the pillows on the floor. Picking it up now, she pulled at the piping, getting more agitated by the minute. "I don't know about that. Don't you remember the day I forgot my hay-fever pills? You know which ones I take. You gave me two to tide me over."

"Seldane. Yes, I remember now. But it doesn't mean anything. We do that all the time, and when the prescription comes in, we just deduct the two tablets we advanced to the customer."

Denise ran her hand through her long hair in a nervous gesture. No wonder she looked unkempt today. "They questioned me about that day over and over. After a while, I started to feel guilty. Then they got me to admit I wanted Harry for myself and that I never liked Betsy. Hated her is the way they put it."

"Denise, you told me many times that you hate her. You probably said the same thing to other people, and one of them must have mentioned it when they were questioned. But I don't understand what this is all about. Harry is the one who died, not his wife."

"They think I killed him so Betsy couldn't have him."

If the situation hadn't been so serious, I would have laughed at the melodramatic implications. "That's ridiculous," I said. "Do they think it took you all this time to make up your mind to kill him? It must be at least a year since they married."

"It was last October."

"All right. October. Do they really believe you brooded about their marriage for ten months and then decided to kill him."

"But you see, Ruthie, they think we remained lovers and I couldn't stand it anymore."

"And that's even harder to believe. Why would he marry a beautiful young woman—excuse me, I have to be brutally frank now—and continue an affair with you?"

Denise laughed and came out with the kind of impish remark that usually made her such good company. "Ask Princess Di's biographers that one."

"Yes, but you're free. If their assumptions were true, Harry could have married you any time before last October."

"I think we're both too exhausted to think straight. Let me make some coffee." I followed her into the kitchen where she quickly put two cups of instant coffee into her microwave and a plate of chocolate-chip cookies on the table. I was glad to get the coffee; even instant would help tonight.

As I drank my coffee and munched on cookies, I thought about the entire bizarre story. It just didn't make sense to me.

Denise sat across the table, stirring sweetener into her coffee. "I don't understand it," she said. "Why do they suspect me when Harry's children and Betsy all have motives?"

"Maybe the police are questioning everyone the same way. Maybe that's what they do when they have no leads."

"What happened to innocent until proven guilty?"

Since I assumed the question was a rhetorical one, I didn't try to answer her. I started to worry that the police would be waiting for me at the pharmacy in the morning. But I had nothing to hide except some long-ago daydreams. I was thankful I'd never said anything against Betsy, not only because of Denise's experience today, but also because she was Michael's daughter. Michael's daughter—I still hadn't come to grips with that knowledge.

I pulled myself together, realizing the selfish turn my thoughts had taken. "Did the police say anything about further questions for you?"

"No, but I'm worried. I always believed if you kept your nose clean, you'd be okay. Now I'm not so sure about that."

"Denise, you know you didn't harm Harry," I said firmly. "And I know you didn't. You can't be a serious suspect."

She was twisting strands of her hair now. "I haven't told you everything," she said. "There's something I just can't talk about."

Nine

Thursday I was on the day shift again and half expected to see either Michael or the police when I arrived at Food Go. But it was surprisingly quiet. My first customer came in twenty minutes after I opened, which gave me time to catch up on paperwork.

Detective Frank Moreway arrived an hour or so later. I was on the phone, trying to solve a difficult problem. The patient wanted a refill of Vasotec, 5 milligrams, to reduce his blood pressure. He didn't have the original vial or the prescription number, so I looked him up in the computer. Then I pulled the hard copy, handwritten by a Dr. Thomas; but when I called Dr. Thomas's office, no one had heard of the patient. Now the office nurse had put Dr. Thomas himself on the phone, and I was listening to an indignant denial that Mr. Rosofsky was his patient.

"But Dr. Thomas, the script is handwritten on your blank."

"I don't care how it's written; he's not my patient."

At that point, a man in a dark suit, incongruous for Scottsdale in August, had stepped up to the window and shoved his I.D. at me. I recognized the name. Detective Frank Moreway was Joey's brother-in-law, and I smiled and held up my hand to indicate I'd be right with him. He glared at me, obviously not used to waiting when he wanted to talk to someone. Now I had another problem: doctors are not accustomed to being put on hold, and here was a Scottsdale police detective who didn't want to wait either.

The patient chose that moment to reappear and yell at me. "I never heard of Dr. Thomas. Just give me my blood pressure medicine. I don't need you to raise my pressure."

"Sir, I can't refill your Vasotec without the doctor's okay. He has no record of you, and now you tell me he's not your doctor."

Frank Moreway, in a deliberately polite voice, interrupted. "Can we hold off on that for a minute, ma'am? I need to get back into the pharmacy and look up some records."

"Detective Moreway, you can come back now." I indicated the door and went to open it for him. "I'm sorry, but I must finish with this gentleman before I can call up any records for you on the computer."

The customer's face had turned red and he was shouting at me again. "Don't give me excuses. I want my medicine."

I sighed. "Sir, this is the original prescription. It's handwritten on Dr. Thomas's form and signed by him. He never heard of you and you never heard of him, so we're at an impasse here." I showed him the prescription.

"I don't care what you say," he shouted. "I go to Dr. Birmann, not Dr. Thomas."

Suddenly I saw what had happened. "Sir, both of those doctors are in the same office, and they cover for each other on vacations. Let me call the office again and see if they can find your record under Dr. Birmann."

So I did and they did. The customer admitted he'd seen some other doctor last time, apologized profusely, and thanked me for straightening things out. I filled his Vasotec, told two other people that I'd have their prescriptions in half an hour, and turned my attention to Frank Moreway.

"I want a printout of every prescription Harry

Stokes got since the beginning of this year," he said. "Also, I have a list of other people whose records I want to see."

He handed me a list that included Betsy Stokes, Richard Stokes, Nancy Stokes, Sheila Stokes, and Denise Seaford. I ran all the names through my computer and saw that Harry's children were not our customers. While the computer printed out the records for Harry, Betsy, and Denise, I tried to talk to Frank Moreway.

"I don't understand, Detective, I thought Harry Stokes died of natural causes."

For someone who, at least according to Joey, gossiped so much at home, the detective was surprisingly laconic with me. "I'm not permitted to discuss the case, ma'am. Just give me the records, and I'll get out of your way."

I indicated the printer and tried to lighten the situation. "If I could invent one that works faster when people are in a hurry, I'd be rich."

"What time are you off duty?" He glanced briefly at a young woman who had come up to the window. "I have some questions, and I don't want the public listening in."

I could feel the color leaving my face even though I knew I hadn't done anything wrong. Leaning over the printer as if to check it, I tried to hide my reaction from Frank Moreway. But I was sure he'd noticed. Stop being foolish, I warned myself. Straighten up and act your age.

"Detective, I'll be glad to answer any questions, but this is a retail business and there'll be people around even at five when my shift ends."

"Isn't there an office here?"

"Yes, but employees will be coming and going all the time."

He gave me a look that I interpreted as suspicious. "Then you have two choices. I can go out to your residence or you can come to police headquarters."

I dawdled with the printouts while I thought this

over. Going to the police department could be embarrassing, but it might be even worse if he pulled up in front of my house in a patrol car. "I'll come to you," I said.

"Fine. Just ask for Criminal Investigations and someone will direct you."

"About five-thirty?" I couldn't help making it a question and waited for his approval.

"Five-thirty," he repeated and left with the printouts.

All day I dreaded the coming interview. Surely my private daydreams had no bearing on the case. He just wanted to discuss the prescriptions with me. But my uneasiness never subsided.

At five I walked over to the Food Go employee restrooms, where I carefully brushed my hair, trying to neaten the wayward curls caused by the humidity, and reapplied lipstick. Luckily I had worn my taupe-and-white geometric-patterned dress, which was less frivolous-looking than some of my other summer outfits. I needed all the self-confidence I could muster.

When I arrived at police headquarters and was directed to Detective Moreway's desk in Criminal Investigations, my nervousness increased. Maybe I'm just reacting to Denise's story, I thought, and tried to calm myself.

Frank Moreway offered me a chair and sat on the edge of the desk, looking down at me. For the first time, I noticed the brown shoes and socks he wore with his dark blue suit. I considered it a sign that he didn't know everything and relaxed slightly just before he led me through a description of every drug on the printouts. Or maybe I just became more professional as we entered my own sphere of knowledge.

First we discussed the four prescriptions that Harry Stokes regularly filled at Food Go. I explained the significance of the increased dosages of Micronase and Lopressor. "But you really should talk to his doctor," I suggested. A noncommittal grunt was his only response, which I interpreted to mean he'd already done so but wasn't going to give anything away.

"Let me be sure I've got it all," Frank Moreway said. Then he had me repeat everything. It was hard to equate this man with the brother-in-law that Joey admired so much, although I was fairly sure repetition was a ploy to see whether I changed any information.

After we went over Harry Stokes's prescription record several times, the detective began to question me about how well I knew Harry. "I knew him only as a customer," I said.

"How often did you see him outside of Food Go?"

"Never."

"You were at his funeral," he said flatly.

Here was another dilemma, but I was not going to make things worse for Denise. "He was a very good customer; I wanted to pay my respects."

Too late. I realized that Joey had heard the entire conversation when Denise urged me to go to the funeral with her. Well, this was my story and I would stick to it.

He surprised me by not pursuing the subject. Instead he went on to Denise's prescriptions, which were pretty straightforward. In addition to her regular script each month for sixty Seldane, which she took for her allergies, the record showed one for Seldane D last month when she had a bad summer cold. I'd cautioned her not to take both drugs at the same time but to use only the Seldane D until the cold symptoms eased off. I remembered thinking it would be simpler and cheaper if her doctor told her to buy Food-Fed, Food Go's brand of pseudoephedrine, a decongestant that doesn't require a prescription, and take it along with the allergy drug.

"No birth control pills?" Frank Moreway asked.

I felt my face flush. "This is the complete record. You saw me pull it from the computer."

"Couldn't the record be altered?"

"Yes, I suppose it could be, but you're welcome to

look over the hard copies—paper copies—of the prescriptions. Anytime."

"I might just do that," he said and began to question me about Betsy Stokes' prescription record.

One glance at her printout and my shocked expression was enough to alert Detective Moreway. "What is it? Was she taking something unusual?"

"No. Nothing unusual. I just didn't suspect . . . I mean, Harry was so much older . . . that is . . ." I was silent.

"You might as well stop trying to hide things from me. I haven't been to *her* doctor yet, but I'm sure he'll cooperate."

I was too disturbed then by the prescription record and his assumption that I was holding back information to notice the tacit admission that he'd talked with Harry Stokes's physician. "I'm not hiding anything," I said indignantly.

He got down from the desk and loomed over me. "Well."

"She's taking Stuartnatal 1 + 1. The other pharmacist filled the script, so I didn't know until now."

"In words of one syllable," Frank Moreway said slowly, "I want you to explain what that means."

"Stuartnatal 1 + 1 is a prenatal vitamin."

His face still had a puzzled expression, or maybe that was a ploy, too, so I hurried to explain. "Betsy . . . I mean Mrs. Stokes . . . is pregnant."

"And why the shocked reaction? You must fill hundreds of prescriptions for prenatal vitamins."

"It's just the circumstances," I lamely excused myself.

He wasn't going to let that one get by. "What circumstances in particular? That her husband was a senior citizen?"

I winced at this term. But then again, to a young man like Frank Moreway, it must have seemed a natural distinction. My mind raced as I tried to absorb the implications of Betsy's pregnancy. Any lingering doubts about suicide were gone, and I thought the likelihood that Betsy had murdered her husband was also diminished. Then I remembered Denise. If she knew about the pregnancy, would the police consider it her motive? In view of the direction of their questions, this seemed likely. I couldn't believe she was a murderer, and I was not going to help them harass her.

"You haven't answered my question," Detective Moreway said.

I couldn't remember the question and must have looked blank. "Why does her pregnancy shock you?"

"Detective Moreway," I said firmly, looking up at him. "I'm trying to cooperate with you in every way possible." Despite the air-conditioning, I could feel sweat trickling down my forehead. It was a normal physical reaction during the Arizona monsoon season, but I was afraid he'd attribute it to a guilty conscience.

He resumed his perch on the edge of the desk. Ordinarily I would have enjoyed talking to him rather than sitting home alone in front of my television. He wasn't really handsome, but his strong features and confident manner would make him attractive to many women. And how often did any young man waste more than a few minutes talking to me? I was just another one of Scottsdale's "seniors." We were as indistinguishable to most young men, and women too, as the palm trees outside.

"All right, ma'am," he said finally. "Let's look at the other prescription drugs that Betsy Stokes gets from you."

The printout showed her scripts in reverse chronological order, with the latest at the top of the page, but nothing unusual had caught my eye until I reached the prenatal vitamins. Now I started from the beginning and looked over the rest of Betsy Stokes's recent medical history for Frank Moreway.

Her first prenatal exam had probably been on July 18 because she'd gotten the Stuartnatal 1 + 1 that day. On July 24 her doctor had prescribed penicillin and Tussi-Organidin DM. "She must have caught the summer cold that's been going around," I explained.

"Is it safe for a pregnant woman to take those drugs?"

"Her doctor prescribed them."

"That's no answer."

Why was he so antagonistic? No one had called Harry's death murder; yet he seemed to be suspicious of everyone. "The doctor writes them and I fill them," I said.

"And if you think the doctor made an error?"

"Then I call him, or her, and check it out." All at once, I was tired of acting like a victim. It was time to confront Detective Moreway. "I don't understand," I said. "Betsy Stokes is very much alive. What does her summer cold have to do with anything?"

I stood in front of him now, all my nervousness suddenly gone. "It's not what the doctors prescribe for pregnant women that I worry about. It's the nonprescription drugs people buy over the counter." I gathered the printouts and handed them to Frank Moreway. Then I adjusted the straps of my taupe leather shoulder bag, giving him time to insist on further questions. He looked surprised but said nothing.

"If you want to have a philosophical discussion on the subject some time, I'll be glad to give you my opinion. But pharmacists don't get a lunch hour at Food Go, and it's nearly eleven hours since breakfast." Half expecting him to call me back, I left the room at a carefully moderated pace and walked to my car.

Ten

I didn't recognize Richard Stokes when he came up to the pharmacy window the next afternoon. This balding man of thirty-five or so, in a forest green and white rugby shirt, bore little resemblance to the conservatively dressed mourner at the funeral. He rapped on the counter even though he could see I was right there.

"In the electronic age," he said pompously, "I guess you can see everyone's prescriptions right away."

"You mean fill them right away?"

"No, I need a list."

Usually they wanted lists of all their prescriptions at income tax time, not in August. I was about to make sure that's what he really wanted when he was joined by a mousy-looking woman.

"Miss," she said in a hesitant voice. "My husband has to have a record of every one of his father's and stepmother's prescriptions."

Maybe it was the association of father and stepmother, but now I recognized Richard and Nancy Stokes. This is turning into farce instead of tragedy, I thought grimly. Who's going to ask for the printout next? Let's see, Harry had a daughter and there's her fiancé. Soon we'll get the maid and the milkman.

"Sorry, I've already given that record to the police." I don't know why I said that. Probably just tired of the pushed-around feeling.

"Don't tell me the police are finally going to do something," Richard Stokes said.

Almost simultaneously his wife's expression showed traces of fear. "Now see what you've done," she shrieked at him.

"Will you stop it?" he said to her through clenched teeth.

"You always say that. Why don't *you* stop it?" She was crying now and pulled a wad of yellow tissues from her purse to dab her eyes.

"Wait for me outside," he said.

Like a child, she wailed, "It's too hot to wait outside." But then she turned and walked awkwardly away from the pharmacy. I didn't know what to do or say, so I busied myself at the computer, trying to act as though I hadn't witnessed the miserable scene.

"Are you getting me the records? That's for Harry Stokes and Betsy Stokes."

"Prescription records are confidential."

"I know that," he said. "But I told you they're for my father and stepmother."

"Then they have to request the records."

"Don't be stupid. My father is dead."

Just what I needed, some customer abuse. That's when I get very polite; that's when I get so polite, it's almost insulting. "Sir, we have a firm policy not to release such information." I articulated each word clearly as though I were speaking to someone with weak English skills.

"I'm getting the store manager," he said and moved quickly away.

Great, I thought. The customer is always right, so how is my manager going to get around this one.

I tried to concentrate on answering the phone and taking care of patients at the window while I waited to see what would happen. Meanwhile I thought about pharmacy law: was it specific on the subject or would I have to explain the ethics of the situation to my manager and hope he'd take my side. He was usually good about supporting us, but I worried just the same.

Richard Stokes returned alone about fifteen minutes later. He spoke now with the voice of reason. "I'm sorry I lost my temper," he said. "Father died last week and I'm sure you realize how upset we are."

"Yes, of course," I said, trying to sound reasonable in return but determined not to release confidential information.

"Well, his death was unexpected. You probably know that he had a few minor ailments."

Although I hadn't heard diabetes and high blood pressure called minor ailments before, I tried to keep an interested but noncommittal expression.

"Now we need the records to see what Dad was taking."

"Can't you just look at his prescription bottles?"

He hesitated. "Look, I see you're good at keeping confidences, so I'll tell you the problem. Dad remarried last year, and we can't . . . I mean his wife won't . . . That is, we don't want to disturb her when she's grieving."

"Oh, I see."

"I knew you'd understand. And we need her prescriptions because . . . well, she's so distraught that we're afraid she might . . . you know, do something foolish."

Either the family was unaware of Betsy's pregnancy or he thought I didn't know. I must have looked skeptical at his last statement, because he finished lamely, "It happens, you know."

I wasn't going to let him off that easily. "What happens?" I asked.

He put his face right up to the window, assuming a solemn expression. "Suicide," he whispered.

"You can't mean that. She's a young woman with her whole life ahead of her." I watched him as I tossed the platitude. He looked angry again and I was prepared for more nasty comments, but he controlled himself.

"All of us are concerned about her. She doesn't eat or sleep, and she never leaves the house."

That's a good story, I thought, but aloud I matched his serious tone. "I'm really surprised to hear that." I paused for effect. "Her father doesn't seem to worry about suicide."

Again his face darkened in anger and I hastily excused myself to help another customer. When I turned back to Richard Stokes, he was ready with another tactic.

"I see you're too clever for me, so I'll have to tell you the truth, distasteful as it is to wash our dirty linen in public."

He would definitely win any cliché contest. I answered two phone calls and then waited to see what he'd say this time. He looked around to make sure no other customers were nearby.

"My wife and I, and my sister as well, believe my father was either driven to suicide or murdered."

As though this were news to me, I gave an appropriate gasp. It must have seemed realistic enough to him, for he continued. "My father was in perfect health. Yes, I know, he had diabetes and high blood pressure, but that's all the more reason why he should have lived to a ripe old age."

Definitely a cliché artist, but I listened patiently while he described a study that was supposed to show "people in our level of society" with such diseases lived longer because they sought medical care earlier and more frequently than the average person. "And my father took care of himself. He never missed taking his medications."

"Yes, he seemed careful about his health," I said.

"So, now you understand why we want the prescription records."

He's so transparent, I reflected. If Harry Stokes had been murdered, this is one person who couldn't have done it. He had plenty of guile, but his words and body language were overdone.

The pharmacy was quiet for the moment, so I decided to play, too. "No. I really don't understand."

Now he was exasperated. "Look here, miss," he

started to say and caught himself. The voice of reason returned. "It's simple. We think Father's death wasn't from natural causes."

"Yes . . . ?"

"So we think he took something or was given something that killed him." He folded his arms and tried for a sincere look this time. "Now you know. I can't say it any clearer."

Sure you can, I thought. You can come right out and say you think his wife was responsible for his death. By asking for her prescriptions, you intimated it anyhow.

"And you've already told the police about your suspicions."

Another glare was his only response.

"I guess that's why Detective Moreway came in for the records yesterday." I tried to sound as if the thought had just struck me. My acting skills probably were no better than his, but I left him no choice.

"Yes. I suppose so."

"Well, in that case, the information is in good hands." I worded all my comments to support my original insinuation that the records were no longer in my possession. It didn't work.

"Don't you still have copies in the computer?"

We had circled to the original impasse. When three more prescriptions came in, I turned away hoping Richard Stokes would give up and leave, but he waited until I was free again. "I'm sure you want to see justice done," he said this time.

Yes, and no news is good news and a bird in the hand is worth two in the bush, I said to myself. "That's exactly why I cooperated with the Scottsdale Police Department." I couldn't resist it: "The ball's in their court now."

"Naturally, I have complete faith in the authorities," he said.

"In that case—"

"Let me finish, miss. You probably don't know this,

but the Stokeses are an old Arizona family. We come from pioneer stock, self-reliant folks, and I'm not waiting for the police to find out who's responsible for my father's death."

"That's strange. I understood you were the one who brought the police into this in the first place."

Now I'd done it. The rage he'd been trying to control burst like water spurting from a garden hose. "You think you're clever," he shouted. "All you ladies with careers are the same. Do you think they fire lady engineers? No, I'm the one who got axed, but the ladies kept their jobs." He glared at me so threateningly that I drew back in alarm. "Pardon me, the *women*. The *women* don't have to worry every time there's a layoff. They're needed to keep the government off the company's back."

I waited for him to run down, but he seemed to be venting the accumulated hatred of years. Although I'd had abusive customers before, this general condemnation of female professionals was something new. I thought I understood what was driving him, but I didn't know what to do. Customers came to the window, heard him shouting, and edged away. I had to calm him.

"Mr. Stokes," I said. He didn't seem to hear me but kept shouting, repeating himself without winding down. "I'm trying to help you."

Finally he stopped shouting and looked directly at me. "You're not helping; you're part of the problem."

I wondered whether it had all been an act. If he were really so disturbed, would he be back to clichés again? "Mr. Stokes, last night I spent two hours at police headquarters going over the prescription records of your father, Betsy Stokes, and . . . others. I suggest you see Detective Moreway and discuss all of this with him."

His expression became even more filled with hatred. If he had a weapon, I was sure he'd use it, and I prepared to drop to the Mexican tile floor behind the prescription counter. "Maybe we've been suspecting the wrong person," he said. "After all, you have more access to poisons than anyone else."

Eleven

All day I tried to convince myself that Richard Stokes's accusations were ridiculous; no one could possibly believe him. But I thought of Denise and the way the police had hammered at her. If they suspected Denise because of a friendship that, to their way of thinking, gave her access to the pharmacy—who would believe me? Their suppositions about her interest in Harry could apply to me, too. I thought how awkward it would be, even though they could never prove anything. And, my inner voice said, how embarrassing if Michael were to hear of your romantic fantasies.

Stop being so foolish, Ruthie, I told myself. I tried to be logical about it. Despite a prescription department full of drugs, I had no idea how to kill a person. If anyone supposed I had a motive for murdering Harry Stokes, did they really believe I could have dropped arsenic or strychnine in his coffee? I relaxed a little at this idea—we didn't even have arsenic or strychnine in the store. Not only that, I'd never had coffee or anything else with Harry Stokes.

But would Frank Moreway believe me? An accusation of murder was a serious charge, and he'd have to investigate. On the other hand, Richard Stokes had already accused his stepmother. Surely, if he showed up at police headquarters today and accused someone else, he would lose whatever credibility he'd had.

I couldn't afford to let someone like Richard Stokes unnerve me. Since Bob's death, I'd become used to coping alone, and I was stronger for it. But this was no ordinary predicament; I needed advice, and I didn't know where to turn. I couldn't bother Denise; she had her own troubles. As for my other friends, I didn't relish telling any of them I might be a murder suspect. There's Michael, I thought. And I knew he had been in my mind all along.

When I got home from work that night, I ran through possible conversations with him. The next day, Saturday, was my day off this week. I could invite Michael for lunch or dinner. No, that might give him the wrong impression; it was better just to ask him over to talk. If he demurred, I would add details. Otherwise I preferred to say nothing on the telephone about Richard Stokes and his accusations.

Possibly Michael had gone back to Tucson by now. I had heard nothing from him since our dinner three nights ago. But surely his daughter still needed him, and somehow I didn't think he'd leave town without saying goodbye to me.

I dialed, expecting Betsy Stokes to answer the telephone—after all it was her home I was calling—so when I heard Michael's voice, I forgot my carefully prepared words. "This is Ruthie Kantor . . . I mean Ruthie Morris."

He laughed and that deep, joyous sound brought back the old memories, but I refused to let myself get caught in the past again. "You didn't have to give a name," he said. "I recognized you right away."

"I wasn't sure you were still in Scottsdale."

His voice sobered immediately. "Yes, of course, I'm still here."

Why was it so hard to ask him to stop by tomorrow? It wasn't a date. And if Michael suspected an excuse for seeing him again, he'd soon discover the real reason for my call. I closed out the schoolgirl reactions and invited him.

Michael said he'd drive over as soon after eleven

o'clock as possible. "I have something to do earlier, but I should be finished by then." I gave him my address and directions. Like the Stokes home, mine is on a cul-de-sac that makes it hard to find.

After we said our goodbyes, and despite telling myself over and over that this wasn't a social call, I checked to see what refreshments I had on hand. Coffee, that's all you need to serve, I insisted to myself. But that was an error in the opposite direction, for any friend or neighbor who came to the house would be offered cake or ice cream along with a cup of coffee. I always kept a raspberry or lemon danish log and two flavors of ice cream in my freezer, just in case. Embarrassment would come not from too much hospitality but from treating Michael less cordially than anyone else.

I fell asleep that night before I'd decided what to wear. During the long Arizona summers, I usually preferred shorts and knit shirts on my days off. Even though I still looked reasonably well in shorts, I decided on a pale blue sleeveless dress instead. The air-conditioning would be blasting away anyhow, and I'd feel more comfortable that way.

In the morning I quickly straightened the house, trying to look at it through Michael's eyes. The Gorman prints Bob and I had bought over the years added color to the champagne walls and dark traditional furniture, and I was proud of my collection of old pharmacy beakers from Dad's store, grouped on end tables and shelves throughout the house. I knew my birch kitchen contrasted sharply with the sophistication of Betsy's starkly modern one, but I had no idea whether Michael's taste was similar to that of his daughter.

He's only an acquaintance now, I told myself. Maybe we can be friends, but expecting anything else will only lead to disappointment. And be honest, while it's pleasant to dream of might-have-beens, we're both different people now.

Michael arrived just after eleven, and I tried to

seem calm as he followed me into my living room, but I knew my face was flushed and my eyes were too bright. We settled across the room from each other; he sat on the turquoise-striped sofa and I went to one of the turquoise-and-peach floral armchairs. I was glad he hadn't taken the other armchair, the one I still thought of as Bob's, because I didn't want to compare Bob and Michael. Michael had been my first love, but Bob had been my husband for more than thirty years.

"At least one worry is gone," he said. "I took Betsy to her doctor this morning and everything's fine."

I didn't know whether to acknowledge awareness of her pregnancy, but he continued before I could react. "She's in her third month, and she was desperately afraid of losing the baby. But, of course, you probably knew about the pregnancy before anyone else."

"Actually I didn't know until I looked at her prescription record two days ago. Tim, he's our other pharmacist, must have filled the Stuartnatal 1 + 1."

"Yes, I know Tim Barnard," he said drily.

"That's right. He was at the funeral."

Michael didn't want to talk about Tim. "Surely you must have guessed when you saw us buying a stuffed elephant at the mall."

"It never occurred to me."

"Didn't you think it a bit unusual for her to be buying toys at such a time?" He didn't wait for my reply. "Betsy was so unhappy that I wanted to whiz her out of that house. I'm sure you know talk and sympathy only go so far."

I could feel my eyes fill and I turned away from him. The conversation was too intense, and I looked for an escape. "Can I offer you some coffee and cake?"

Michael must have understood, for he said that coffee sounded great and followed me into the kitchen. As I stood at the turquoise Corian counter, my back toward him, he continued.

"I thought a tangible link to the future might help, so I suggested buying toys for the baby. Maybe it was a silly idea, but it seemed to work until we met you and that nosy neighbor of Betsy's."

"Denise is okay," I assured him.

"Possibly, but she always seems to be around when we leave the house or pull in again."

I had regained some self-composure now and hurried to defend Denise. "She's a good person, Michael. I value her friendship."

"Okay, forget I said that and tell me what's worrying you." He reacted to my startled look by assuring me he could still sense when something was wrong. Again I resolutely shut out the past and concentrated on telling Michael of my encounter with his daughter's stepson. I tried to keep a neutral tone and subdue my emotions.

Michael surprised me again. He did not adopt the easy tactics of reassurance and insist that Richard would talk but not act. Nor did he make light of my unease and embarrassment.

"You're right, Ruthie. He could put you in a difficult position professionally."

"And personally," I added.

"Yes. Although I think he'd have to offer some proof that you and Harry were seen together other than at Food Go." By this time, we were seated at my kitchen table with untouched cups of coffee and plates of danish pastry in front of us.

"Harry was a friendly type. Are you sure you never did see him outside of the store?"

I got to my feet, indignation fueled by the knowledge that I would never tell him about my daydreams. "You know I'm not a liar."

"Indeed, you've always been painfully honest."

"Then, why . . . ?

"Because I can tell that you're holding back something."

"Well, if you must know, you're right," I burst out. "He was a handsome man, and he and I were both alone, so I imagined he'd ask me out. It was a fantasy.

He never noticed me as anything but his 'friendly neighborhood pharmacist.'" I phrased the last words sarcastically.

Michael jumped up, too, and took my hand. "I'm sorry," he said. "I didn't mean to push you into confidences. And it's nothing to be ashamed of. If we were all held accountable for fantasies, they couldn't build prisons fast enough for everyone." He moved away from me, picked up our two coffee cups, and nodded toward the microwave. "Why don't I reheat these?"

Two minutes later we sat at the table again, sipping hot coffee. We talked about Michael's work. He was on unpaid leave from his job as director of a busy hospital pharmacy. He managed four full-time pharmacists and three technicians, and the hospital administration was being very supportive, using part-timers to fill in for Michael.

"I'd like to hijack Betsy back to Tucson for a time, but she wants to stay here."

"Let her do it her own way," I advised. "Sometimes people mean well, but they don't realize we need to adjust to living alone in familiar surroundings. Otherwise we face a second bereavement when we do return."

His intense look warmed me. "You had to go through it all alone, didn't you?"

"Betsy's so much younger," I said. "At least Bob and I had many years together. And these suspicions of suicide or murder—that must make it much harder."

"You've been drawn into this mess, Ruthie, and you should know what's been happening. Let me clue you in."

I refilled our coffee cups and listened, half afraid of what he would say, but glad that I'd finally hear facts instead of rumors.

"I'm sure you know from his prescriptions that Harry had diabetes and high blood pressure, so we expected his doctor to certify either one or both as the cause of death. But he refused to do it." Michael, who had always seemed so sure of himself, looked disconcerted.

"Of course, we wanted to know why, and we were told that both conditions had been under control. Neither was considered life threatening in Harry's case." Michael continued to look uneasy.

"But his physician couldn't be sure of that."

"I know, and before we could challenge him, the son and daughter claimed Betsy had driven their father to suicide."

"Why?"

"You've met Richard. Does he strike you as a rational person?"

I laughed despite the serious turn of our conversation. "You know what they say—even paranoids can have enemies."

"They've made things very difficult for Betsy. I guess it's to be expected when the stepmother is younger than the children of the first marriage."

"And even when she isn't," I said.

"That's probably true in some cases." His intent gaze was directed toward me again. "I won't insult you by asking for promises of confidentiality, but I want to tell you about my daughter's situation. Too many people have misjudged her."

I put my elbows inelegantly on the table and leaned forward. He paused for a moment as if to collect his thoughts, or perhaps he was still hesitant about revealing too much.

"After the divorce, Betsy lived with her mother from the time she was five until just after her ninth birthday. She was with me every other weekend and for a month in the summertime. And I talked to her on the telephone nearly every day.

"Then her mother remarried and moved to London, and Betsy came to live with me. But those formative years . . . I know what the shrinks say about needing a father figure. When she became serious about someone a little older than me, I guess I should have expected it."

"Are you saying it was a complete surprise?"

Michael took a moment to reflect, although I was sure he'd already considered the facts many times. "Before Harry, her few serious relationships were with men in her own age group, like Tim Barnard," he said. "Yes, I was surprised. In fact, I didn't expect it to last.

"Betsy always talked about a large family; she missed having siblings." He smiled ruefully. "Well, I was wrong about one thing. I told her Harry was too old to give her a child."

"Do the Stokes family know she's pregnant?"

"I'm not sure. She isn't on close terms with them. They haven't treated her very well—innuendos about marrying for money. That sort of thing."

"Even grown children find it hard to believe their parents are attractive to others," I said.

"Maybe that's part of it. But I think it's more like projection."

Michael's coffee cup was empty again, and I quietly refilled it without interrupting him. He went on, slowly, as if weighing every word. "I don't enjoy discrediting my daughter's family by marriage, even though they haven't acted like family."

I thought it was time to help him along. "What exactly happened?"

"Betsy tells me they were constantly trying to get money from Harry. Not small loans either. You may not know that Richard lost his job recently. He wanted his father to be his venture capitalist."

"He expected Harry to finance him in a new business?" Even Denise hadn't seemed aware of this turn of events.

"Yes, Richard and his wife badgered him incessantly. They tried to make him feel guilty about remarrying. And the daughter was just as relentless."

"I thought she was doing well in real-estate sales."

I'd heard all about Sheila's wonderful career from Denise.

"But not well enough to help her boyfriend buy the jazz club where he works."

It looked like they all viewed Harry as a cash machine. I wondered whether Betsy had wanted anything special for herself. They'd certainly spent a bit on remodeling the house, but that might have been Harry's idea.

Michael again anticipated my thought. "Betsy loved him, and all she wanted from him was a family."

"Suspicion of suicide is bad enough," I said, "but now that they're talking of murder, what will happen?"

"The police are probing in all directions. If they had anything concrete to go on, something would've happened by now."

"As long as we're being frank with each other, Michael, I have to tell you I did hear suicide mentioned. But as soon as I knew about the baby, I figured they were wrong; he had everything to live for."

Michael's expression changed, a strange look that I couldn't read. He said nothing, so I went on. "And you? Do you think it was suicide?"

"I don't know."

This answer surprised me, for Michael had just told me how much Betsy wanted the baby. I wondered if Harry Stokes had reacted differently to the news.

"I guess I should tell you: when my daughter's pregnancy was confirmed, Harry wanted her to have an abortion."

"An abortion! But you just told me how much she wanted children."

"Yes, she did and she still does. On the other hand, Harry's family is grown. He has grandchildren. He said he was past that stage in life; he didn't want to start all over again with a baby that would be mistaken for another grandchild."

Michael's eyes seemed to ask something of me, but

I couldn't decipher his meaning. He paused and then spoke in a rushed voice, as though he wanted to get the words out as quickly as possible.

"I may as well be frank with you. They argued constantly about it from the time they knew about her pregnancy until his death a couple of weeks later."

Twelve

I stared at Michael. So much for my psychological insights. "I thought Harry would be happy about the baby. Some older men would be proud to have a pregnant young wife."

"Perhaps, but he should have thought of the possibility before he married Betsy. It's a mistake to marry out of your generation."

Was he sending me a message or was my imagination misinterpreting his words. I reverted to the original subject.

"You said you're unsure about suicide. Does that mean you think murder is a real possibility?"

"I don't know."

He had surprised me again. I'd expected a vehement denial because suspicion of murder would be far worse for Betsy than whispers of suicide. "Was there any evidence?"

"Ruthie, the police haven't told us much. My daughter found her husband collapsed on the floor next to their bed. There was no suicide note. And the autopsy showed no sign of poison."

"Then aside from Harry's doctor, what's the problem?"

He turned away and studied my sunlit peach-and-turquoise kitchen without expression. After a moment, he seemed to reach a decision. "I guess I'd better tell you everything."

I waited for him to continue, too unnerved to comment. The only sound in the room was the air conditioner as it cut in automatically. Without knowing why, I felt chilled enough to want to raise the thermostat temperature.

"As you know, Harry's death was sudden and completely unexpected. The reason I wanted to know what medications he was taking—there was a box of 12 Hour Food-Fed, your store's brand of pseudoephedrine, by his bedside table."

"Surely he knew enough to avoid decongestants with his heart condition."

"They weren't his tablets; they were Betsy's."

I stifled my exclamation of surprise. No wonder she was suspected of contributing to her husband's death. Food-Fed is an OTC, a drug sold over the counter. No prescription needed. It's effective in clearing cold symptoms and making it easier to breathe at night. Many people with clogged nasal passages take the longer-acting twelve-hour tablets at bedtime so they can get a good night's rest. I knew that Food-Fed, taken with Harry Stokes's other prescriptions, was contraindicated because it would act as a cardiac stimulant. Betsy also would have known because of the warning on the package.

Michael's tone was even, but I could see how troubled he was. "Betsy had the cold symptoms first, and she was taking the Food-Fed. When Harry began experiencing the same discomfort, he must have taken her pills."

"Are you sure that's what happened?"

"We don't really know. But Betsy says she only used four tablets. Then she started worrying about the baby and checked with her gynecologist. He okayed the Food-Fed, but meanwhile she felt better and decided not to use them anymore."

"How many were left in the box you found on Harry's night table?"

"One."

I winced. Each box contains twelve tablets, which

meant Harry must have used seven of them. For anyone else, Food-Fed would be a good choice to relieve nasal congestion. With Harry's physical problems, it was not. His doctor should have advised him never to use that kind of stimulant, especially since the dosage of his blood pressure medication had just been increased. No wonder the police were asking so many questions. But why did they examine Denise's record if a nonprescription drug contributed to Harry's death? It didn't make sense.

"The whole thing is unbelievable," I said.

"And frightening, too. Betsy insists that she had no idea Harry was taking her decongestant. She tells me she put the unused pills in the medicine cabinet and forgot all about them."

"But when Harry's cold symptoms began, was she the one who suggested the Food-Fed?"

Michael looked uncomfortable. I thought I'd hit upon the truth, but I was wrong. He started to speak, hesitated, and then began again. "They weren't on good terms during the last weeks of Harry's life. In fact, they were barely speaking to each other except to argue about the baby."

"She must feel terrible now."

"It's been a nightmare." He met my eyes and held them. "I know I sound like a father defending his daughter, but she loved him very much. And, Ruthie, he loved her. Betsy was convinced he'd change his mind about the baby."

"This entire situation is so strange, Michael. No one could be sure that the decongestant would kill him."

"That's what I told the police, but Detective Moreway says if it hadn't worked, the murderer might have tried something else."

"Murderer!" My voice sounded hoarse to me. "Then they really believe Harry was murdered?"

"That's one of the possibilities they're investigating. There's no way to prove his heart gave out because he took or was given a cold remedy that overstimulated his heart. And there's no way to prove Betsy didn't give him her pills. On the other hand, we can't show he died of natural causes, and the uncertainty makes everything worse for Betsy."

"What are you doing to help her?"

"I haven't been able to accomplish anything. It's unbearably frustrating to wait for others to act."

"And I didn't help when I refused to give you the printout."

He smiled at me. "I wasn't trying to make you feel guilty. In any event, the printout didn't change Detective Moreway's suspicions."

"I think," I said slowly, "it's all right to reveal that Harry wasn't taking anything you don't already know about."

"That's what I was afraid of."

"Afraid of?" I echoed.

Michael gathered our dirty cups and saucers and carried them to the sink. "You see, my daughter's trained me to an active role in kitchen duties."

I got up and stood beside him. "I'll just pop everything in the dishwasher."

"Good. I didn't really relish washing dishes."

"Okay, Michael," I said, getting back to the pertinent conversation. "Level with me."

He seemed surprised at my firm tone, but answered readily enough. "I've been hoping Harry's doctor had prescribed something that would explain his death. No, that's not right either. What I want is a discovery that will vindicate Betsy."

"And implicate someone else?"

"If that's what it takes."

"What if the 'someone else' is innocent? After all, I'm one possible 'someone else.'"

Michael took me gently by the shoulders. "No one in his right mind would suspect you."

"Now, we're going in circles. If I agreed, I wouldn't have asked for your advice."

He had the grace to look embarrassed. "Ruthie, there's no evidence against *anyone*. Anyone at all. I know this police investigation is difficult for you and Denise. Maybe for Harry's children, too. But it's far worse for Betsy. We're talking about a newly bereaved young woman, a pregnant widow."

I sympathized with Michael and his daughter, but I couldn't suppress the thought that she might be guilty after all. Fathers are not the best judges of their daughter's moral fiber and, if Betsy were a murderer, her father would probably deny it even after justice was done.

"This is all supposition," I said. "No matter how much we talk about natural death versus suicide versus murder, we'll probably never know the truth."

"I must find out whether Harry was murdered."

"How?"

"I haven't worked out the details yet," Michael said. "But I know I never wanted anything as much as I want this grandchild. And I'm not going to let Betsy suffer like this through her pregnancy."

Anxiety for Michael made me shudder. "It could be dangerous for you."

"That's precisely the point. If I can seem to know too much, the murderer will come after me."

Thirteen

After Michael left, I could only replay our conversation. I'd expected him to calm my fears; instead, my turmoil had increased. I changed into a bathing suit, grabbed my Mace canister, and went out to the pool, hoping some exercise would help.

As I opened the patio doors and stepped outside, a blast of hot air made me gasp. I reached for one of the beach towels hanging on the patio and carefully placed it and the Mace on the stone bench beside the pool. Some of my friends tease me about the Mace, but since Bob's death left me alone, I worry about someone climbing the back fence into the pool area.

The pebbled surface around the pool, supposedly cooler than cement, was too hot to walk on in bare feet. I ran quickly to the deep end, jumped in, and did thirty laps before I had to rest. Thirty laps sounds terrific, but for my pool size, it's not much. I once read about a seventy-eight-year-old man who swam his age in laps every day, but I've never reached my own magic number without long breaks in between.

Although the pool water must have been about 100 degrees, it revived me and I sat on the patio, more relaxed than I'd felt in days. Suddenly my fears seemed exaggerated. The sudden death of someone in his sixties with diabetes and high blood pressure was more likely to be a natural occurrence than suicide or murder. It wasn't surprising that the police thought in terms of the latter, but I refused to go along with their scenario.

I decided it was foolish to worry about Michael. There was no murderer, so the trap he intended to set would never spring. I understood Michael's anxiety for his daughter, but it was misplaced. Nothing would happen. Police inquiries would go nowhere, and eventually Michael would return to Tucson.

That certainty stopped me for a moment. If you want to daydream, I told myself, go ahead. But know that it's only a pleasant way to pass a sultry summer afternoon.

After a time, the heat drove me into the water again, and I passed the rest of my day off alternating between pool and patio. I spent most of the evening in front of the TV, my usual Saturday-night pattern since losing Bob. Sunday was a workday for me, so I turned in early, with only a brief thought about Harry Stokes's death before I fell asleep.

At the pharmacy, Sunday was usually a quiet day. Unlike the rest of the store, it was only open from nine to five. I worked alone, but was able to catch up on paperwork and transmit a huge order to the wholesaler for delivery the next day. Mondays were always busy, and anything I could do in advance would make life easier.

I didn't see any of the people involved in the Stokes case, if you could call it a case. Denise was working the late shift in the coffee shop, and none of Harry's relatives showed up demanding confidential prescription records.

I still felt relaxed when I opened up on Monday. My first customer shattered this calm mood. The problem was her insurance plan, which wouldn't accept her card when I ran it through our machine. I sympathized with the customer until I became the target of her anger. She was a thin woman who didn't look like she had the lung power to explode the way she did.

"What do you mean it won't take?" she screamed.

"I've got a sick child out in the car, and I need his antibiotic."

"Out in the car?" I couldn't contain myself. "Surely not in this heat."

"You mind your own business and give me the medicine."

I explained again that I couldn't put it on her insurance plan, but she could pay for it now and try to collect from the insurance company later. While I tried to straighten out this problem, more customers arrived at the window. Both phones rang continually, and I tried to keep sane until ten o'clock when my technician would arrive. One thing about Joey, he never wasted a moment when he came in or waited for me to tell him what to do.

The next time I glanced at the clock, it was close to eleven. Where was Joey anyhow? He was hardly ever late, and I really needed him today.

By noon I was convinced he'd caught the summer cold that was going around, but why hadn't he phoned in? I called Greg Blackstone, the store manager, on the intercom.

"I think Joey's sick," I told him. "Can you get me one of your people to fill in?"

He promised some help and eventually sent a young woman from the cosmetic counter. She'd never worked in the pharmacy before but quickly took over the phones and the cash register, which allowed me to concentrate on filling prescriptions. From time to time, I wondered about Joey and whether I should call him at home. Better not, I told myself. He's responsible enough to call in as soon as he can.

Just before one o'clock, Denise appeared at the pharmacy. "Where's Joey? I wanted to talk to him before I clock in."

"I don't know where he is."

"Did he hear anything new from his brother-in-law?"

"I couldn't tell you," I said impatiently. "He hasn't shown up today."

"Okay, don't get upset. I recognize busy people when I see them." She turned to leave.

I assured Denise I'd see her later at the coffee shop and returned to the prescription backlog, without time to spare her another thought. When she reappeared a few minutes later, I tried to hide my annoyance. I noticed she was dabbing at her eyes with a tissue.

"Ruthie, let me into the pharmacy. Hurry!"

I unlocked the door for her and had just time enough to guess that her allergies must be acting up before she grabbed both my arms. She was sobbing now, the tears running unchecked and ruining her makeup.

"I telephoned," she said. "They told me . . . Oh, God, I can't believe it . . . they told me he's dead."

Without conscious thought, I knew who she meant, but the words wouldn't form. I waited.

"He drowned in that damn fountain. How could it happen? Little children drown in swimming pools here. It's in the papers all the time." Her sobs were louder now. "But Joey was twenty years old. He couldn't drown like that!"

Even though I'd known, her words hit me so forcibly that I doubled over, holding on to the counter for support. I cried along with Denise, the customers at the window forgotten.

"When?" I whispered.

"Sometime during the night. The maintenance crew found him this morning." She choked up and couldn't continue.

I pictured that beautiful fountain at the Franklins' condominium complex. How would Joey's parents ever be able to look at it again? I thought of Joey—so eager to learn, so avid to be a part of everything.

But I couldn't grieve for him now; I had to help all the people who needed their medications. Many of them were in pain, too. I had to pull myself together.

Motioning to the relief technician, who was staring at us helplessly, I asked her to take Denise to the employees' lunchroom. Once again I called Greg Blackstone on the intercom.

He appeared almost at once, breathing as if he had run all the way. "Ruth, what's happening here? At least three customers reported something wrong in the pharmacy."

I explained briefly, trying not to break down again. His shocked expression showed he hadn't yet heard. "Okay, I'll try to get someone here. When is the other pharmacist due in?"

He turned to the waiting customers. "Folks, the pharmacist isn't feeling well. There'll be a slight delay in filling your prescriptions, so why don't you do your grocery shopping meanwhile. We'll take care of you as quickly as we can."

Some of the customers murmured sympathetically and handed their prescriptions to the store manager, but I heard one grumble that he couldn't wait. "You go and take a break," Greg told me. "I'll stay here and run a holding operation."

Legally, a licensed pharmacist must be in the pharmacy at all times, but I didn't argue with the manager. I grabbed my handbag and ran to the customer restrooms, not wanting to see other Food Go people in the lunchroom. By now Denise would have told everyone. I couldn't bear to hear them discuss Joey's death over and over, adding details even if they had no real information.

The shocking news and Denise's abrupt way of relaying it made me feel as if I'd been kicked in the head. And every minute my head ached more as I thought of poor Joey. I splashed cold water on my face and reached into my handbag for aspirins. After a while, I forced myself to return to the pharmacy.

"I phoned your staff pharmacist. He'll be here as soon as possible," Greg Blackstone said when I let myself into the pharmacy. He had a telephone receiver in each hand and looked more harried than usual.

"Thanks. Why don't I take one of those calls?"

He handed the nearest receiver to me, and I took

down a prescription for Erythromycin, an antibiotic. "Look, I don't want you giving out drugs while you're in this shocked condition. You take the phone calls and I'll be the people person."

I was trying to regain some semblance of my professional self and at least hold on until Tim could arrive, but my mind wasn't functioning clearly and I realized Greg was right.

Tim Barnard came rushing into the pharmacy shortly afterwards. "What's wrong?" he asked. "You said we had an emergency."

"I didn't want to break it to you over the telephone," Greg told him. "We've had terrible news—it's Joey Franklin."

"Joey? Is the kid sick?"

"No, Tim. He's dead."

Tim looked as shocked as I felt. Maybe I should have suggested that Greg Blackstone call in a relief pharmacist from another Food Go, one who didn't know Joey. But I hadn't been thinking clearly.

"What happened?" Tim asked. "Was it a traffic accident?"

"We don't have any details, only that he was drowned."

"Those kids are always rafting on old tires. I told Joey a couple of times it's too dangerous."

"Don't jump to conclusions," Greg said quietly. "The main question is whether you feel up to taking over here. I want to send Ruth home."

"I feel terrible, too, but Ruthie is . . . was a lot closer to Joey. I can manage okay." He turned to me. "Can you drive yourself home? Maybe the store could spare someone to drive you."

I assured both Tim and Greg that I could get home by myself. "But I'm worried about Denise," I told the store manager.

"That's my next job. I figured the pharmacy's needs had a higher priority than the coffee shop's."

I wanted nothing more than to go home alone, crank up the air-conditioning, and burrow into the bedclothes. But I couldn't desert Denise. "If you can spare her, I'll take Denise to my house."

"Go ahead." Greg looked toward Tim Barnard, who was already at the window, talking to customers. "It looks like the pharmacy is under control."

He took my arm and walked me to the employees' lunchroom, where we found Denise crouched over one of the lunch tables, her head buried in her hands. Two other Food Go employees, a woman from the bakery and one of the meat cutters, were trying to calm her.

Greg Blackstone went to the water fountain, filled a paper cup, and walked over to Denise. "Here, drink this," he said in an authoritative voice he seldom used.

She took the cup and stared at it. I thought she must be in shock, but when Greg repeated, "Drink this," she drained the cup.

"Give her something stronger when you get her to your house," Greg said. "If she still seems dazed, call a doctor."

As disturbed as Denise was, his decisive manner produced results, and I realized, not for the first time, why he was an effective manager. Denise got up and, with one of us gripping each arm, walked out of the store.

At her first exposure to the bright sunlight, she pulled her arms away from our supporting grip and covered her eyes. "Her pupils must be dilated enough to be painful," I told Greg Blackstone. We led Denise to my car and Greg helped her in, even buckling her seat belt for her. Then he helped me into the driver's seat, asking again if I was sure I could manage. I fastened my own seat belt and reassured Greg, but I was finding it hard to believe I could drive the five miles to my home.

Take it slowly and concentrate, I told myself. There won't be much traffic. You can do it. I pulled out of my parking space carefully, knowing Greg was watching, and headed for the shopping-strip exit.

The drive home seemed interminable. I tried to turn my thoughts away from Joey and my friend who sat beside me whimpering; I made no attempt to speak to her, convinced it would only make it harder for me to get us home safely.

When I pulled into my driveway, I wondered how I'd get Denise into the house without help. She was in the same trancelike state, but she followed me inside without resistance.

It was cooler in the house, but not cool enough, and I started toward the thermostat to lower it. "I'm cold," Denise mumbled before I moved more than a few feet.

Shock, I thought. I led her to my guest bedroom, opened the sofa bed, and helped her off with her shoes. "I'll be right back with some blankets," I told her.

The blankets were packed away for the summer, and it took me a few minutes to collect two of them. I put one over Denise and told her to let me know if she was still cold. "I'm going to make you some hot tea."

"Thanks," she said.

I figured it was an encouraging sign; she wasn't completely out of it. My own shock was mitigated by the need to help Denise, and I quickly heated two cups of tea in the microwave. While the microwave was going, I found some pillows and propped her up so she could drink the tea. I added lots of sugar to both cups, put them on a tray and returned to her.

She sipped the tea, and I saw some color return to her face. "Thanks," she repeated.

"Should I try to get you to a doctor?"

"No, I'm doing better. I'm not so cold anymore."

I observed her closely. She wasn't shivering, which I took as a good sign. Her eyes seemed more focused, although she kept them closed most of the time. But they were probably still hurting; she'd been crying for the better part of an hour.

"It was the way they told me. I was so unprepared. Well, I guess you're always unprepared." She picked up the cup of tea again. I noticed she'd moved the covers back a little, so she must be warmer. The perspiration was running down my own face, and I mopped at it with a tissue, wishing I could adjust the thermostat.

"Some stranger answered the phone, not one of the Franklins. I thought it must be one of Joey's friends, and I asked to speak to him." Denise started to cry again. I silently passed along the box of tissues I was using.

"There was no warning, no attempt to lead up to bad news. 'Joey's dead,' he said. 'That's a stupid joke to play on me,' I yelled. But I think I knew. 'It's no joke, lady. I wish it was,' he said. And that was that."

I wondered if it was better to keep her from reliving that telephone call, but I realized she had to talk. "How did you get the details?" I asked quietly.

"I don't know. He must have told me."

"His parents were so proud of him," I said. The lump in my throat seemed to thicken, but I controlled the tears that threatened. It would only make everything worse for Denise.

I thought about Joey again. When Bob died, my world had fallen apart. But in its own way, this death was as devastating. A young man of twenty, and one that I would have been delighted to have as a son. I felt bad when Harry Stokes died, but he was really only a casual acquaintance. Joey and I had worked side by side for nearly two years.

Something flashed into my mind when I thought of Harry Stokes. Was it too much of a coincidence for Joey to die so soon after Harry? I pushed the thought away, convinced there was no connection. Harry's death, as far as anyone had been able to prove, resulted from natural causes. From what Denise had discovered, Joey's death was a terrible accident.

The connection between Harry Stokes and Joey was too tenuous. Now, if Michael had been the victim of a drowning accident, I told myself, that would be suspicious. Michael had been setting himself up to trap a nonexistent killer. *His* death would have made murder a plausible assumption.

Fourteen

Eventually Denise fell asleep. She didn't hear the phone when Greg Blackstone called to see how we were doing, and she didn't awaken when Tim Barnard called to ask about a prescription that had come in earlier that day. I looked in on her from time to time, but mostly I sat in my kitchen, drinking iced coffee and thinking about Joey.

My mind kept returning to thoughts of murder even though I'd already decided there was no rational basis to connect the deaths of Joey and Harry. One possibility kept nagging at me. If Joey's brother-in-law had been right, if Denise . . . No, I refused to consider it.

But I couldn't drive away the suspicion. I would have to think it through. Frank Moreway had questioned Denise and then me about the possibility that she got something from the pharmacy and used it to kill Harry. He knew Denise and I were friends and surmised that our relationship gave her access to the pharmacy.

I had no doubts about my own actions: Denise couldn't have gotten any such drugs from me, either overtly or covertly.

Now I had to consider Joey. Was it possible he had allowed Denise into the pharmacy? Again I was certain this had never happened when I was on duty. And Tim never let anyone into the pharmacy, not even the store manager.

We did have a few relief pharmacists who filled in for days off and vacations. But it hardly seemed likely they'd even know Denise, let alone invite her into the pharmacy.

And my thoughts careened head on into the same wall they'd hit days ago. We had nothing for a murderer to use. The times when someone could buy arsenic to kill mice or weeds or whatever were long past—if they'd ever existed outside of fiction.

I suddenly felt ashamed of my suspicions, but I knew I had to work them through before facing Detective Moreway's inevitable questions. A detective who refused to accept Harry Stokes's passing as a natural occurrence would be relentless in probing his own brother-in-law's death.

Now I'd come full circle. After convincing myself the two deaths were unconnected, why was I so sure Frank Moreway would take the opposite view?

I went to the refrigerator and got more ice. The house was hotter than I liked it, but I was afraid to cool it down. Denise was still asleep, wrapped in the blanket, and I figured she would have kicked it off if she were too warm.

No one else telephoned. Twice I started to call Michael but hung up after pushing two or three numbers. I considered phoning one of my friends just for someone to talk to, but there was no one else I wanted to share my worries with.

At about 5:30 in the afternoon, Denise came into the kitchen. Her eyes looked swollen, underlined by dark smudges where her makeup had run. With her uncombed hair and creased dress, she seemed very different from the impeccably turned-out woman I was used to seeing.

"I'm sorry, Ruthie. It must be awful for you to have me on your hands right now."

"Stop apologizing. You would do the same for me."

"That's just the point. You were even closer to Joey." Her voice shook when she said his name, and I was afraid of another crying jag. She clenched her teeth and went on. "I should have been helping you over the shock, not the other way around."

"You did help me. You gave me someone else to think about."

Denise shook her head but was quiet. I offered her a sweater if she still felt chilled, but she insisted she was better.

"What can I fix for dinner?"

She started to protest. "Denise, the best thing we can do is spend some time together and talk it out. Otherwise, we'll each eat alone and be even more miserable."

"Then let me pitch in. I make a great salad."

"Okay, just take whatever you need from the fridge. I've got oil, vinegar, and cans of tuna and anchovies in the cabinet by the window."

I took out the gray placemats; they matched my mood. On second thought, I added napkins with a peach and gray floral design. No reason to make dinner any gloomier than I expected it to be.

While Denise tore apart a head of lettuce she found in the crisper, I arranged slices of cheese and rye bread on a platter. Then I started a fresh pot of decaffeinated coffee. We took our time over the light meal, not saying much at first.

Denise suddenly put down her fork. "We've been avoiding the subject. We need to talk."

"There isn't much to say."

"Yes, there is. I was awake for a while before I came out to find you. Going over everything." She stared across the table as if wanting to pull words from me.

I obliged. "Everything?"

"Let me ask you, Ruthie. Haven't you noticed how strange it all is?"

There was no way I could tell her about my suspicions since she was their object. So I played dumb. "What do you mean?"

"Two deaths in less than two weeks."

"People die every day. Every hour. Even more often."

"These two people knew each other."

I let my eyebrows show skepticism. "It's the shock, Denise. You're still not thinking clearly."

"I'm thinking very clearly. First Harry, then Joey. It can't be a coincidence."

It was hard to contradict Denise when I'd considered the same possibility. But I felt it necessary to dispel her morbid ideas. "They only knew each other casually."

"You'd be surprised. They talked a lot."

"Joey and Harry Stokes?"

"Why do you think Joey wanted to tag along with us to the funeral?" She stopped for a moment, and I knew she was thinking we'd be going to another funeral now.

"I don't know. I figured he wanted to pay his respects because he knew Harry as a customer."

"Ruthie, twenty-year-old boys don't worry about paying their respects."

"Well, maybe he was curious."

"Curious about what?"

"He probably overheard us talking about Harry and Betsy and that whole situation."

Denise helped herself to more salad and reached for the pepper, covering the entire surface of the salad. I'd seen people in the southwest eat this way since my childhood in Tucson but had never picked up the habit. She seemed to be marking time while deciding how much to tell me.

"A few times when Joey was on the late shift, he'd have lunch in the coffee shop first."

"Well, that's nothing unusual. Many Food Go people do that."

"Yeah, but why would he have lunch with Harry Stokes?"

I thought over this piece of news. What did the two of them have in common? It was an unlikely combination. "You tell me, Denise."

"Joey was trying to get money from him."

"What?"

"You don't have to shout at me. I'm not trying to say anything bad about Joey—not blackmail or anything like that."

I forced myself to laugh. "You do have a vivid imagination."

She was angry now. "You always say that. But I've been right before, and I know what I'm talking about. Maybe I don't have much education, but I . . ."

"Please, Denise, I wasn't trying to put you down."

"I'm sorry. It's hard to make sense of what's happening, but I need to tell someone. You know how small the coffee shop is, so I couldn't help overhearing them."

"You don't have to apologize. Just tell me, and I promise not to interrupt again."

Denise, when she got down to it, gave the details concisely. She had forgotten about those lunches until this afternoon, but she was sure they represented a connection between the two deaths. "Joey wanted a loan to help with his college expenses. He said it was too hard to work so many hours at Food Go and get good enough grades for medical school."

"Yes, he did talk about medical school all the time."

"His family lives comfortably, but Joey's always had to help out with tuition and his other expenses."

"I know that. But why would he expect Harry Stokes to finance him?"

"It was supposed to be a business deal. They would have a lawyer draw up a note and Joey would return the money with interest to Harry or his heirs."

"Why didn't he just get student loans the usual way?" I asked.

"That was Harry's question, too. Joey said student loans are more difficult to get nowadays."

"And how did Harry react to all this?"

"It was hard to tell, Ruthie. I heard him turn Joey down, but they continued to lunch together and discuss it."

"You and I must be the only ones who didn't want money from Harry Stokes," I said.

Denise's summer tan suddenly turned an unbecoming reddish brown. I looked at her in surprise. "You, too?"

Her eyes wouldn't meet mine but were fixed on the last bits of lettuce and diced tomatoes on her plate. "I wanted to become a dental technician," she mumbled.

"You never told me."

"I got the idea from Joey. I mean, I had the dream for a long time but no money to make it real."

I didn't know what to say. All I could do was thank God that Detective Moreway didn't know about this aspect of Denise and Harry's relationship. He was digging for information, suspecting an affair, but here was another strong motive for revenge.

"Maybe it sounds tacky when I put it this way. But I kept thinking that I'd known Harry for years. If he was going to help anyone through school, it should be me."

"Yes, but why should he? He had his own family to think of." I nearly mentioned the expected baby but stopped myself in time.

"It would have been strictly business. I made the same offer as Joey—a legal note, interest, the works."

I sighed. It seemed a lot of people were playing Harry like a private Arizona lottery. "Why not take an equity loan on your house and use that money?"

"There's no way I could make the extra payments."

"Then how could you have paid Harry back?"

"The arrangement would have been to start paying back as soon as I finished and got a good job," Denise said stiffly.

It sounded unrealistic to me. As far as I knew, dental technicians didn't make all that much. "What did Harry say?"

"He told me everyone was after his money."

"I guess they were."

"His children never paid back. They got money from him for years. Called it a loan each time, until he finally got wise and refused to give them more."

"You mean after he remarried."

"Probably."

"Denise, did you and Joey approach him recently?"

"You don't have to be so tactful. Why not ask me straight out if it was before or after he married Betsy?"

"Okay, was it before or after?"

"It was two months ago." She refilled our coffee cups, acting as hostess in my kitchen, or maybe she was just used to refilling coffee cups.

I found it hard to meet her eyes. "Does anyone else know all this?"

"Maybe."

"What does that mean?"

"I think he told Betsy. She started avoiding me around that time."

In this, my sympathies were with Betsy, but I couldn't say so. I wondered whether hearing about her from Michael's point of view had influenced me. "I don't know what to say, Denise. If Detective Moreway questions you again, it might be better to tell him the truth before he hears it from someone else."

She looked even more upset. "That's what worries me."

"Let's sit in the living room and talk. And if you're warm enough now, I'd like to lower the thermostat."

Denise started to clear the table, but I insisted it was more important for us to talk without interruption. So she followed me out of the kitchen and waited while I detoured to the thermostat, lowering it to 68 degrees.

"Give me your opinion, Ruthie."

"I just did."

"No, not about telling Detective Moreway. About what's been happening."

I tried to keep my voice as calm as possible. "We

can't have an intelligent opinion until we know more about how Joey happened to drown in that fountain. There may be a simple explanation."

"Let's check the local news tonight. Maybe they'll have something about it."

So we talked of other things until it was time for the news. I turned on the TV, and we watched world and national news, sports, the weather. I really didn't expect to hear about Joey, but it was the first local item. And the police were investigating his death as a suspected murder.

Fifteen

Neither of us said a word. We sat and watched the screen, mesmerized by the police spokeswoman who explained that it was impossible for an adult to fall into the fountain accidentally and drown. We saw a close-up of the familiar fountain and watched her point to the height of the curved edging.

"What if he were sitting on the edge and fell in?" the reporter asked.

"You can't sit on the edge. Look at the design." A well-known Scottsdale architect now appeared on screen to explain that the fountain was deliberately scalloped, to keep children from hopping onto the rim and walking it.

"Could he have hit his head and fallen in?" the reporter asked.

"The matter is still under investigation," the police spokeswoman said stiffly. "We have no further information at this time."

Hints about caring for your pets in the monsoon season came on next, and I turned off the set. We stared at each other. Although it was Denise who had talked of murder, she now seemed more surprised than I was.

"It can't be," she said over and over.

"It didn't sound like they have much to go on. Maybe that was just TV hype."

"The Franklins live in a gated complex." She went

on as if I hadn't said anything. "You saw the security guard; no one could get by him and kill Joey."

"We don't know what really happened."

"Yes," Denise said. "It's too soon."

We were both silent for a time, until Denise asked me to run her back to Food Go so she could pick up her car, assuring me she would have no trouble driving. She was over the first shock.

I did as she asked. We had very little to say to each other as we rode to the store. At the parking lot, I let her out alongside her car, said good night, and hurried away. All my suspicions had returned, and I wondered if trying to get money from Harry Stokes was what Denise had avoided telling me that day the police questioned her. In any case, I could find no rational explanation for her contradictory behavior.

Trying not to think about Joey or Denise, I drove home slowly. As I approached the house, I could see Michael's silver-and-gray Lexus in my driveway. He was leaning against the side of the car, his hair silvery in the moonlight. I was so glad to see him that I had to concentrate very hard on parking my own car.

"I was afraid one of your neighbors would suspect me of burglary and call the police."

"Are burglars driving Lexuses these days?"

He grinned at me. "I'm glad you're okay; I was worried about you."

We walked into the house together and settled in the living room after Michael refused my offer of coffee. "How is your daughter?" I asked him.

"About what you'd expect until today's news hit."

"Yes. I figured you were here because of Joey." I tried to keep my voice steady, but it caught as I said his name.

Michael took my hand and held it for a moment. "It must be very tough for you. Have you . . . had you worked together long?"

"Nearly two years. He was a good kid." Despite what Denise had revealed about his attempt to borrow money from Harry Stokes, I still believed this.

Then why are you so hard on Denise for the same thing, I asked myself. She's a mature woman; she should know better, I thought.

Continuing to argue with myself, knowing that I'd never had her money worries, I missed what Michael was saying. "I'm sorry. My mind keeps wandering."

"That's understandable." He was so comfortable to be with, not judgmental like some of my friends. "I asked if the police contacted you."

"No," I said and paused. "Not yet." I told Michael how few details we had and how Denise had broken down at the news.

"I whizzed back to Tucson yesterday and stayed overnight. Picked up my mail, checked that my job was still waiting. Other errands like that. This afternoon, when I heard the news on my car radio, the name didn't mean anything. But then I picked up a Phoenix station, and they said he worked in a Food Go pharmacy."

Michael reached for my hand again. "Ruthie, they're calling it murder."

"Do you think there's a connection?"

He didn't have to ask the kind of connection I meant. "Remember what I said the other day, that I want the murderer to think I know too much. Maybe Joey really did know too much."

I wondered if Michael also suspected Denise, but assured myself he didn't know enough about her. "Who do you think . . . ?" My voice trailed off.

"Either Richard Stokes or Sheila's boyfriend."

To hide my relief at not hearing Denise's name, I jumped up and turned toward the kitchen. "I need something cold to drink. What about you?"

He said he preferred water, so I filled two glasses with ice cubes and filtered water and brought them back into the living room. Michael was standing by the white baby grand piano, looking at the two framed photographs I keep there—my wedding picture and another of Bob and me on our silver anniversary.

"You both look very happy," he said and moved back to his seat on the sofa.

I sipped the cold water but was silent, thinking about the contrast between his own marriage that had ended in divorce and mine that had ended in death. I could see Bob so clearly, sitting in this room, an audience of one, eyes closed and expression absorbed, as I played his favorite piano concertos. For all the piano lessons I'd had as a child and teenager, I was only mildly competent. But Bob always enjoyed my playing and wouldn't allow me to criticize myself.

I forced my thoughts to the present. "Why do you suspect those two?"

"They're the most likely candidates. I told you they were after Harry's money."

"Yes, but murder . . ."

"Someone did it. I thought so all along, but now with Joey's death, I'm convinced."

"Michael, remember that course in logic we both took when we needed credit in the humanities? Just because one event follows another, it doesn't mean they're connected." I tried to concentrate on the Latin expression for faulty causation, but couldn't think of it.

"This is not a case of 'post hoc, ergo propter hoc,' " Michael said without a pause.

"After this, therefore because of this," I translated. "That's what I meant."

"Can you think of any other reason for Joey's murder?"

"Robbery."

"I know we have muggings in Arizona just like anywhere else. But I really doubt this was one."

"You may be right. I'd guess most muggers would avoid an area with guarded gates."

"Was he involved with drugs? I mean illegal ones?" He saw my look of astonishment and backtracked. "That was a stupid question. You'd never have kept him as your technician."

"That's probably the first thing that comes into

people's minds these days when a young person is murdered," I said. "When I think of his parents, I'm just overwhelmed."

"Did he know Harry?"

I hesitated. No way was I going to destroy Joey's reputation by repeating secondhand information. "Harry was often in the store. We all knew him."

"Only as a customer? Are you sure?"

Now I was angry. "You sound like Detective Moreway. There was no reason for anyone to kill Joey."

"Don't get so upset. I wasn't implying anything wrong."

"You weren't implying anything wrong," I echoed. "First you suggest drugs, then . . . then I don't know what else." My voice faded. Take care, I warned myself; you're on dangerous ground.

"Okay, let's look at it from another direction. Is there something Joey could have learned that placed him in jeopardy?"

"I don't know," I answered truthfully.

"Whatever the reason for Joey's death, I'm more determined than ever to trap the killer."

"Why put yourself in danger? If the two deaths are connected, you don't have to worry about the accusations against your daughter; she's out of the picture now."

"What do you mean?"

"Even Detective Moreway wouldn't believe a pregnant woman could sneak out in the middle of the night and drag a strong young man into that fountain."

Michael rose from the sofa and paced across my living room. "Unfortunately, Betsy has no alibi, since I was in Tucson last night."

And that means you have no alibi either. The thought leaped into my mind without conscious deliberation. I wondered how I could suspect someone who had once been so important in my life.

Sixteen

After Michael left, I went over our conversation. He'd made it clear he was only trying to anticipate how the police could interpret the situation. He still seemed to believe he had to find the murderer to remove suspicion from his daughter—and from Denise and himself, I thought. And from me, too.

If I had these crazy ideas, what did other people think? Michael was right; we couldn't fully trust anyone until we learned who was responsible for the two deaths.

Now I realized I no longer doubted. If Joey had been murdered, he was not a random victim. Somehow he'd acquired dangerous information, and it had to be about Harry Stokes. Nothing else made sense.

I turned this over. What could Joey have learned? The police had investigated the prescription records of Denise and of everyone in the Stokes family. But not his father-in-law's, that persistent inner voice said. Michael's pharmacy record would be down in Tucson.

Be logical, I cautioned myself. If they're in Tucson, Joey wouldn't have had access either. And besides, Michael had probably been in Tucson until his daughter needed him, which wasn't until after Harry's death.

But what could Joey have found out that no one else

knew? He was a technician, not a pharmacist. Well, that didn't mean anything. A good technician, and he'd been one, could pick up quite a bit. After two years at Food Go, someone with Joey's inquiring mind probably knew more about the practical aspects of pharmacy than many a senior-year pharmacy student. But I still couldn't see how Joey would be the only one with knowledge dangerous to the killer.

Exhausted though I was, I tried looking at the problem from different angles as I got ready for bed. Because I desperately wanted to believe in the people I cared about, I assumed Denise, Michael, and Betsy were all innocent. Yes, I admitted to myself. I cared about Michael and about his daughter, too. And Denise was my best friend. That left Richard Stokes, his wife, Nancy, Sheila Stokes, and Sheila's boyfriend—whatever his name was. What could any of them have done that Joey discovered? I finally dozed off with the same questions spinning in my mind.

Although I had the night shift on Tuesday and could sleep late, I awoke at six, drenched in perspiration despite the air-conditioning and the ceiling fan over my bed. Even on the hottest nights, I liked to sleep under a light cotton sheet. This morning, one end of the sheet was twisted round and round as if I'd transferred my confused thoughts to the bedclothes.

It was during breakfast that I decided Joey's parents might know something. I couldn't just barge in and ask questions, but as Joey's manager, I should visit them. It would be easier to ask Denise to come along, but I decided to make this condolence call alone.

Here was another thought to be examined. Was I mistrustful enough of Denise to exclude her? No, I assured myself; I just didn't want distractions.

At eleven I passed the fountain and pulled up to the guarded gate at the Franklins' complex. The guard took my name and telephoned for clearance before he raised the electronic arm and let me drive through.

Following his instructions, I made two right turns

and pulled up in front of a two-story pink condo with roof tiles of a paler pink. Just beyond its wrought-iron fence, also pink, I could see Joey's motorcycle in the side yard. A Ford pickup and a late-model sedan were visible in the carport, but no other cars were parked outside. It looked like I was the only visitor, and that's what I'd been hoping for.

Ordinarily I'd have wanted other visitors to help with the small talk. I dreaded this condolence visit to Joey's family, but this could be my only chance for some insight into why Joey was killed. And I needed to remove suspicion of the people I cared about.

A heavyset woman in a sleeveless housedress opened the door. I'd met Joey's parents several times. Although this woman looked familiar, I knew she wasn't Mrs. Franklin.

"I'm Ruth Morris, the pharmacy manager at the Food Go where Joey worked," I told her.

"I know," she said. "Don't you remember me? I get all my medicine from you."

I looked at her again, trying to put a name to the face, but it wouldn't come. For a minute, I was tempted to try a social lie, but I was never good at lying. "I'd like to see Mrs. Franklin," I said.

The flabby face took on a hurt expression. "I'm surprised you don't recognize me. Dr. Ellis calls in all my medicines to you." We stood in the entry hall while I waited for her to ask me in, but she hadn't finished with her grievances. "Because of Joey, I always drove all the way to Food Go. Five other drug stores. That's how many I pass every time. Well," she added plaintively, "I guess I won't bother anymore."

Just what I needed, I thought, as she moved away from the door and I followed without invitation. The pink slate tiles of the entry met deep-pile mauve carpeting in the living room, and I wondered if Joey's mother liked pink or if a previous owner had chosen the exterior and interior colors. I tried to recall how long the Franklins had lived here, focusing on irrelevancies to avoid thinking of what I must do.

Both of Joey's parents were seated on a rattan sofa covered in a floral chintz, the style of furniture I associated with Key West and Ernest Hemingway. Mrs. Franklin's eyes were red-rimmed. She clutched a handful of tissues, and as I walked into the room, she was reaching for another one from a box on her rattan and glass coffee table. Her expression seemed unfocused, and it didn't change when she saw me. I wondered what drugs they had put her on.

"Ruth Morris," I said into the silence and shook hands with her and the dour-looking man beside her. "I wanted to tell you how sorry we all are. Joey was the best pharmacy technician we ever had at Food Go," I added so she could place me.

"Oh, yes. Food Go. Ruthie. Joey always called you Ruthie." The words were choppy and seemed to be forced out of a mouth that trembled when she said her son's name.

"I used to tell him to have more respect," Mr. Franklin said. "Who ever heard of calling your boss 'Ruthie'? I always call mine 'Mr. Williams.'"

Although they were my contemporaries, the Franklins seemed older, which was surprising for a couple whose son had barely passed his teens. On the other hand, their daughter, Detective Moreway's wife, was eight or nine years Joey's senior. I looked around the room, surprised not to see her.

After an awkward pause, they introduced my ex-customer as their next-door neighbor, which explained why there were no extra cars parked outside. I wondered whether I could outstay her, and if so, how I could get the Franklins to talk.

The neighbor offered to make coffee for everyone and bustled off to the kitchen. I could hear her rattling cabinet doors and thought uncharitably about this opportunity for her to examine the contents of every closet.

I waited, very self-conscious, not sure what to say. The Franklins waited, too. When the silence became unbearable, I remembered how people had seemed afraid to talk to me about Bob after his death. Yet I would have preferred reminiscences to stilted conversation and awkward pauses.

"Joey had such a quick mind," I said. "He absorbed information so fast, I sometimes thought he knew more about pharmacy than some of our new graduates."

"He wanted to be a doctor," Mrs. Franklin said and reached for her tissues again.

"I told him to become a druggist," her husband said. "We don't have money for medical school. All those years, and studying so hard he wouldn't be able to earn."

"Joey could've done it." Mrs. Franklin turned to face her husband. "You know he could. Once he made up his mind . . ."

"Well, he liked working in the drugstore. So, I told him to become a druggist."

"He would've been a wonderful doctor."

They seemed to be repeating an old argument, one that saddened me immeasurably. I had to speak. "Joey was good with people. He really cared about them."

"He was always like that," Mrs. Franklin told me. "If I had a headache, if his sister had a cold, he'd wait on us hand and foot. Hand and foot. Most boys aren't any use around a sickroom. But Joey felt real bad if someone was hurting."

"Druggists help people, too." Mr. Franklin wasn't giving up.

"Do you like your coffee black?" the neighbor asked me. Despite her hurt feelings or maybe because of them, she'd taken pains to arrange slices on a tray—something that looked like banana bread interleaved with a darker bread I didn't recognize. She handed cups and saucers to each of us and poured the coffee.

The coffee occupied us for a few minutes, making it

unnecessary to search for topics of conversation. I concentrated on my slice of banana bread, noticing the pink rose pattern of the dishes. The neighbor spoke first. "I have to get home, Edna. I'll look in again later to see if you need anything."

She made no move to leave but sighed as she helped herself to a second piece of the darker bread. "I keep thinking he's going to walk in and tease me to bake zucchini bread for him."

"Yes," Mrs. Franklin said. "Joey always loved your zucchini bread."

I had taken the last forkful from my plate, and it suddenly thickened into a lump that I couldn't swallow. How awful for the Franklins if I choked up here. I made an effort, aided by a quick sip of coffee, and managed to swallow after all. "Did you bake this?" I gestured toward the tray. "It's delicious."

She looked directly at me for the first time since I'd disappointed her at the door, and at that moment, her name burst into my mind. Stephenson, Alice Stephenson.

"Don't you like my zucchini bread? You only had the banana bread."

"Thanks, Mrs. Stephenson." I reached for another slice, thinking of the old joke about the mother who bought her son two shirts for his birthday. He put one on right away only to hear her ask, "What's the matter? You didn't like the other one?"

My mind was playing tricks on me again because I didn't know how to bring the conversation around to the things I wanted to know. And it would be even more difficult with the neighbor listening.

"Alice has been so good to us," Mrs. Franklin said. "I don't know what we'd do without her."

"No more than anyone else would do for you," the neighbor mumbled. She walked over to the sofa, hugged Joey's mother and father, gave me a brief wave, and left the house.

One obstacle out of the way, I thought. As I considered my next move, Mr. Franklin returned to our previous conversation. "Joey would've been a wonderful druggist."

"He knew just how to talk to our customers," I said. "They all liked him."

"That's because he cared about them," Mrs. Franklin said.

We were going in circles, and I was afraid we'd say the same things over and over no matter how long I stayed. And what would I do if their daughter walked in with Frank Moreway? I was trying so hard to figure out how to get information from them that I nearly missed it.

"Really cared about people. Not like most boys his age," Mrs. Franklin was saying. "That man who died a couple of weeks ago. You wouldn't believe how upset Joey was."

"Do you mean Harry Stokes?"

"Yes, that's the one."

"And Joey was upset?"

"He said the man came into Food Go all the time. Of course, it bothered Joey. I told you he cared—"

In my impatience, I cut off the flow of words. "I know he was a caring person, Mrs. Franklin. But how could you tell he was so upset? What did he say? What did he do?"

I was afraid the Franklins would wonder at the strange turn in the conversation, but they didn't seem to find anything odd in my questions.

"He wasn't eating right," Mrs. Franklin said.

"And he talked about the old guy all the time," her husband, who wasn't much younger than Harry, added.

I tried to think back to the day we'd learned of Harry's death. Joey had seemed excited. Then he'd surprised me by wanting to go to the funeral. Had he been upset or worried? I'd been aware of Denise's mood, but I didn't remember consciously observing Joey. After I left the Franklins and had more time to think, I would try to reconstruct those two weeks.

"What did he say about Harry Stokes?" I asked and

held my breath. They'd surely find this question strange.

"He talked about the summer colds or flu or whatever that was going around," Mrs. Franklin said. "When I think how I used to worry about Joey being exposed to all those sick people, and now . . ." Her voice trailed off and she reached for another tissue.

"This old guy had the flu, but he came in for his other medicine." Mr. Franklin made a croaking sound that could have been a laugh and then patted his own bald head. "You probably know he was taking something to grow hair."

So much for patient confidentiality, I thought, but nodded and quietly waited for Joey's father to continue.

"Someone on television or in the movies, I could see it. But to spend so much money every month. And that other stuff, too." Mr. Franklin flushed and stopped talking.

"I never like to take anything unless I have to," his wife added. "Joey said the more you take, the more careful you have to be. Some drugs are okay by themselves, he told me, but they can kill you if you mix them." She looked squarely at me for the first time. "You probably know all that."

"That's why we keep patient records in the computer. Patient profiles we call them." Now or never, I thought, and just as I told myself I had to be more direct to find out anything, the telephone rang. Ordinarily I might have used the ringing phone as an opportunity to say goodbye and escape, but I was determined to learn more from Joey's parents.

Mrs. Franklin excused herself and went into another room to take the call. She was one of those people who pitched her voice higher for the telephone than for in-person conversation. "You don't have to rush over here again. Just rest up." She paused. "Okay, if you want to." She paused again. "No, we haven't been alone. Alice came by. And now Joey's boss is here." Another pause. "Okay, I'll tell Dad."

As I'd guessed from Mrs. Franklin's end of the conversation, Joey's sister would be here soon. "She's expecting again," her mother explained to me. "I don't want her to get overtired."

Now I knew I would only have Joey's parents to myself for a short time. I had to find out as much as I could and as quickly as possible. But what could they tell me that the police, including their son-in-law, hadn't already asked? On the other hand, I had no way of knowing if the police saw a connection between Harry Stokes's death and Joey's. Maybe they weren't asking the right questions. The trouble was I didn't know the right questions either.

I'd learned that Joey was concerned about drug interactions, but so was Detective Moreway when he interviewed me. And Joey's interest might have been awakened by his brother-in-law, rather than the reverse. This family certainly revealed professional information to each other. I wondered whether Joey's sister knew of her husband's suspicions about me and what her reaction had been to the news that I was at her parents' home.

"So you don't really know why Joey wasn't eating right?" I raised my voice at the end to make it a question rather than a statement.

"He cared about people. That's why."

"Yes, of course." I tried it differently. "Did his appetite change all at once or did it happen gradually?"

This time, Mrs. Franklin did look puzzled, but she answered nonetheless. "No, it didn't happen right away. He talked to us about the man that died just the way he told us about a lot of the customers. We liked to know what Joey was doing at work. And he made it interesting."

I said nothing although I blamed myself for not emphasizing confidentiality to Joey. Had he talked about the customers to all his friends, too?

Mrs. Franklin still seemed uncertain, but now I suspected it was because she was trying to recall when

Joey's eating habits had changed. I waited, hoping I could get out of there before their daughter arrived. Not knowing how long it would take her to drive over, I shifted uneasily at the sound of every passing car.

"Don't you remember?" Mr. Franklin asked his wife. "It was the day of that funeral. You thought he was just late for work when he rushed off without dinner."

"That's right. He didn't eat anything before work, so I had hamburgers waiting for him. On those nice onion buns. The ones we buy at Food Go. Joey loved burgers on onion buns, but he said he was tired and went right to bed."

Maybe he was tired and I'm being foolish, I thought, remembering how exhausted I'd felt the night of the funeral. But I was quite a bit older than Joey, and talking to Michael had drained me emotionally.

"Joey said you never had children, so you probably don't know how much a teenage boy eats. Well, he wasn't a teenager anymore." Mrs. Franklin pressed a tissue to her face and was silent, while I sat there hating myself for doing this to her. "But he still ate like one. I used to make all his favorites. He was always rushing off to school or work. And I wanted to be sure he had regular meals."

Mrs. Franklin seemed so obsessed with Joey's eating habits, I couldn't tell how much of her concern was justified. "And he was oversleeping and cutting classes," she suddenly added.

"That's because he was walking around all night," her husband told her.

"You never said."

"I didn't want to worry you. A couple of nights, when I got up to use the bathroom, Joey was sitting here with the television on. Just the picture—no sound."

"Why? Did he say why?"

"He said he was thinking. Listen, I figured it was that girl he broke up with last winter. You know, he wanted to keep seeing her and she wanted to date other boys. Joey was miserable."

"But he got over that," Mrs. Franklin protested.

"They act like they're over it, but it's just an act. I know he wanted to get back with her again. She wouldn't have him."

"She wouldn't have Joey!" His mother was outraged.

"What's the use of talking about that now?" Mr. Franklin rose suddenly and left the room.

I listened to their conversation and suddenly remembered that I, too, had thought Joey wasn't sleeping enough. But I couldn't sort out the details now. It was time for me to leave and I got up, trying to rationalize my terrible intrusion because I was there to help find Joey's murderer. And to clear my friends and myself from suspicion, I said silently.

Before I could take Mrs. Franklin's hand, say goodbye, and go, I heard the front door open and then sharp steps on the entry tile. Joey's sister, whom I'd met once or twice at Food Go, rushed into the room and hugged her mother. Despite my dismay at not getting away before her arrival, I felt some relief that she was alone.

"And you're Ruthie," she said. "It's so nice of you to come."

"I was just leaving."

"No, please don't. It does my folks good to have people to talk to."

So I sat down again, thankful that at least her husband, the police detective, hadn't accompanied her. Carolyn Moreway took the armchair across from mine. "Joey really loved working for you," she said.

I half expected to hear that he should have been a druggist, but Mr. Franklin had not reappeared. "And I was telling your parents he was the best pharmacy tech we ever had."

Carolyn sighed. "You'd think people would be safe in a gated complex. Guard service twenty-four hours a day. And it costs my folks plenty for that."

"Did Frank find out anything?" her mother asked.

"They're still trying to trace all Joey's movements on Sunday. Frank is questioning someone right now."

"I told Frank he was with his friends all day."

"Yes, Mom. Frank talked to all of them. They were hanging out at Bill Reed's, mostly playing volleyball in the swimming pool."

"Did the Reeds invite him for dinner?"

I was trying not to seem too interested in the conversation between mother and daughter, but I wondered again why Mrs. Franklin was so worried about food. Maybe she was right, and I didn't appreciate how normal her concerns were because I'd never had children.

"Bill's parents weren't home. The boys sent out for pizza, but Joey only had one slice. He was meeting someone later for dinner at the Sizzler."

"A girl?"

"That's what Bill Reed and Joey's other friends figured. But it was a man. They didn't remember his name, only that Joey was talking about a customer who died. And this was the wife's father. Frank thinks he was the last person to see Joey alive, and he's questioning the man right now."

Seventeen

I must have gasped, for both women turned toward me. "Sorry," I said and stood up again. "I just realized I'm late for an appointment." With a minimal exchange of polite words, I left Joey's mother and sister. His father still hadn't reemerged, so I asked them to say goodbye for me.

Hot as it was outside, I was glad to get back into my car. The key was unsteady in my hands, but I put it into the ignition on the third try and slowly made my way out of the complex, shuddering as I passed the fountain. I turned into the first side street and pulled over, letting the motor run so the air-conditioning would work.

It couldn't be Michael, I told myself. He had no reason to kill them. But I remembered his eyes when he told me he wanted Betsy's happiness and the grandchild-to-be more than anything else in the world. And Michael had kept after me about the prescription record. Was it to find out how much I knew? Could he have been pursuing the same information from Joey? Maybe he was after Tim Barnard, too. I would have to warn Tim.

Warn people against Michael? I couldn't believe the turn my thoughts had taken. But I knew I must discreetly tell Tim to be careful about revealing professional information to anyone except the police.

This was getting worse all the time. First the police had suspected Denise and, I admitted to myself, at one time I had wondered about her. Now it was Michael.

I gripped the steering wheel but left the car in neutral. Frank Moreway questioned you, too, I told myself. Why are you so disturbed about Michael?

But this was different. Michael had invited Joey out to dinner on the eve of his murder, and I couldn't think of any legitimate reason. As far as I knew, they had never even spoken to each other, although Michael might have noticed Joey at the funeral and at Food Go.

This could all be part of Michael's scheme to bring the murderer into the open by appearing to know too much. But that didn't make sense either, because it meant he'd suspected Joey, which was absurd.

It's only absurd now that someone murdered Joey, I thought. I considered what Denise had told me about Joey's attempts to borrow money from Harry Stokes. What if Joey had been responsible for Harry's death and Michael had found out. Then, in a rage, Michael had drowned Joey.

Michael didn't have rages. He had a very even disposition. Thirty years ago, that inner voice said. How do you know what kind of a man he is today? And there was something else; something Michael had said was bothering me, and I was too upset to figure out what it was.

I forced my hands to a normal position on the steering wheel and moved into drive. Avoiding the heavy traffic on Scottsdale Road, I kept to side streets as much as possible and drove home slowly. My answering machine showed calls from Denise and Tim. Nothing from Michael.

Denise, I knew, would be at Food Go at noon, so I didn't bother returning her call. Her message asked me to see her at the coffee shop before I clocked in, so I'd have to leave for work soon.

I called Tim at the store. He wanted to be sure I

would be there on time, because he had an appointment. After reassuring him, I decided to get to Food Go early enough to eat lunch at the coffee shop and see what Denise wanted. Then I'd still have a chance to sound out Tim and try to urge caution. As for Michael, I wouldn't be able to contact him today, but maybe he'd come into Food Go later. If he had nothing to hide, he might even tell me about his dinner with Joey.

Now I remembered what was bothering me. Michael and I had already talked about Joey's death, but he'd never mentioned the dinner. I tried to think of a reason for Michael's reticence, but each idea that came to mind was more sinister than the one before.

When I arrived at Food Go, the coffee shop was still busy with the lunchtime crowd, but it was past one o'clock and I knew they'd be thinning out soon. Denise brought over my usual tuna salad and iced tea but couldn't stop to talk. I dawdled over the food, waiting for her to have some free time.

After a while, the tables occupied by twenty- and thirty-somethings from nearby office buildings emptied out. Four senior citizens at the nearest table to mine stayed on, but they had finished eating and only wanted their coffee cups refilled from time to time.

Denise walked over with the iced-tea pitcher. "I'm glad you're here. We need to talk." She stood with her back to the seniors and mouthed the words. I could barely hear her.

I shrugged toward the other table. "They're too busy talking to each other to pay attention to us."

"Maybe."

"What's happening, Denise?"

"I'm worried."

That didn't surprise me. Who wouldn't be worried after a co-worker was found murdered, especially since Denise also lived next door to another possible victim?

She remained at my table with the pitcher in her

hand, continuing after a quick glance to be sure her manager wasn't in earshot. "I have no alibi."

"You're being silly now. How could anyone who lives alone be expected to have one for the middle of the night? I don't have an alibi either, but it never occurred to me that I'd need one."

"Well, it should have occurred to you," she told me firmly. "All of us will be questioned. When I think what they put me through when Harry Stokes died ... And this will be worse because this time there's no longer any doubt. A killer is walking around."

"You're being melodramatic again."

"And you're an ostrich with your head in the sand."

I didn't want to quarrel with Denise. And far from worrying about her whereabouts Sunday night and early Monday morning, I could think only of Michael and the contradiction between where he'd said he was and where he really had been.

"Let's not argue, Denise. I just can't understand why you seem to want the police to suspect you."

"I don't *want* it. In fact, I'm terrified." Her voice was still so low that I had to strain to hear the words. "But it's not the police I'm afraid of. What if the killer thinks I saw something Sunday night?"

"At the Stokeses'? What does that have to do with Joey?"

"They always hang around there. All of them—Richard and Nancy, Sheila and her boyfriend—I see them come and go."

"What about Betsy?" I hesitated and added, "And her father?"

"Oh, I don't remember telling you about her father. So you do know he's that good-looking older guy we saw with her at the toy store?" Her disappointment showed as she put the question to me.

"Yes, I know. Someone else told me," I said without elaboration.

"He was gone all weekend. As soon as he wasn't around to protect Betsy, the others started arriving.

First Richard and Nancy. I can always recognize that leased Mercedes of his. Typical of Scottsdale—the guy has no job and he drives a sixty-thousand-dollar car."

I was impatient with her. "What are you trying to tell me?"

"Just that they were arguing with Betsy. She came running across the two driveways to my door to get away from them. And they followed her. It was terrible."

Two young mothers, each with a toddler by the hand, entered the coffee shop, and Denise had to seat them and take their orders. I thought about her story. Although she hadn't had a chance to give me the details, I doubted whether any confrontation between Denise and the Stokes family would be related to Joey's death. Now, if one of their family had been killed that night . . .

I looked at my watch. Time to check in, especially since I wanted to talk to Tim Barnard before he left for the day. As I retrieved my time card and put it into the machine, I wondered whether Denise had seen Michael at all that weekend. Was she really sure he had been away the entire time? Even so, it wouldn't be much of an alibi. If he'd returned quietly from Tucson on Sunday night, he could have easily avoided his daughter's home and the people who knew him.

And then there was Denise. Was she telling me about all the people she'd observed over the weekend to give the impression that she'd been home all the time? Was it a ploy to defuse suspicion about her own whereabouts? More confused than ever about the murders, I unlocked the door to the pharmacy and walked in.

"You're early," Tim said. It was the way he usually greeted me when I was on the late shift.

"You said you had an appointment."

"Yes, well. I do have to leave on time today."

The pharmacy seemed quiet for the moment. Better say what I had to before the telephones started ringing and people lined up at the window for their prescriptions. Still, I hesitated because it was never easy to talk to Tim, and I knew he'd take offense now.

"People have been asking me what we filled for Harry Stokes."

"What kind of people?"

"You know, relatives, the police." I tried for humor. "Sometimes it seems like everyone and his sister."

"Well, you're the manager here. They certainly wouldn't talk to me."

It was a sore point with Tim that I was the pharmacy manager; he had made it clear on more than one occasion that he felt he could do a better job. He wanted to set the schedules, and he wanted to attend store meetings with managers from the other departments. That was one reason why I never asked him to change shifts with me unless it was absolutely necessary.

"I'm not here all the time," I stated.

"Well, neither am I."

"Tim, this is important. I think Joey was killed because of something he found out about Harry Stokes, and I don't want you to put yourself in danger."

"I can take care of myself."

Despite his brave words, I could see that Tim's jaw was clenched. I wanted to make sure he'd be careful. "Joey probably didn't feel threatened either," I told him. "Listen, Tim, I'm trying to figure out what's happening, but meanwhile I felt I had to warn you."

"And the police? Why haven't they warned me?"

"I don't think they've made the connection."

"If the police aren't worried, then neither am I," Tim said.

I turned away to help a middle-aged man at the window. He handed me a prescription for thirty Mevacor, informing me that it was to lower his cholesterol.

"This cholesterol business is nonsense," he said. "My doctor is overreacting."

I wondered what his count was but decided I had no right to ask. He was still complaining as I turned to the computer. Both phones had started ringing, but Tim had already removed his white jacket and was studiously ignoring them. I answered the phones and returned to my customer, who was tapping on the window to get my attention.

"How much will it be?"

I looked it up and gave him the price—"Ninety dollars for thirty tablets."

"No way am I going to pay that much when my doctor just wants me to try them. Give me ten."

"Ten will be thirty-five dollars."

"That's outrageous. Can't you do simple division? Ten should be only thirty dollars."

"Sir, a larger size of most things you buy costs less per unit. The Mevacor is three dollars a tablet when you get thirty, but it works out to three-fifty a tablet when you buy ten."

"Highway robbery," he muttered. "Give me back that prescription!"

As I went to help several more people who'd appeared at the window, I was thankful he wasn't shouting his displeasure. Too bad he hadn't showed up during Tim's shift. I thought about how much I missed Joey. He would have remarked cheerfully that it takes all kinds, a comment I'd heard so often from him. Joey was gone, though, and now I'd antagonized Denise, too.

But Denise didn't stay angry for long. During her break, she came by just long enough to invite me to her house after work. "Some people who want to talk to you will be there," she said. She wouldn't give me any more information, and I was too busy to press her. So at nine o'clock, I went through my closing procedure, clocked out, and drove to her house.

I suppose I expected to see Michael and his daughter there, but instead found Denise's other neighbors, Verna and Raymond Branden, the ones I'd met at the funeral. Verna Branden was a thin, white-haired woman who seemed to take as much interest in the Stokes family as Denise did. She explained to me that she and Raymond were block-watch captains. I could see they were serious about the job.

"So much crime today, you know." She peered expectantly at me, and paused until I nodded in agreement. "We had two burglaries in the neighborhood so far this summer. Of course, both houses are owned by winter residents, so no one was around at the time. Why, if Raymond and I hadn't noticed the broken windows, I don't know what would have happened." This time she looked toward her husband for confirmation.

"The police won't catch them anyways," her husband said, lips curving down in a sour expression.

"Burglary is bad enough, but to have a murder on the block . . . And that Richard Stokes had the nerve to tell me to my face that we're in the block watch because we're nosy." She waited for a reaction from Denise and me, but we said nothing. "Everyone knows we're supposed to check up on all the houses in this cul-de-sac. I don't see other people volunteering to do the job."

"Don't worry, Verna. The rest of us are glad to know you're looking after things," Denise said. "Especially when we have to be at work."

"Everyone thinks when you're retired you have nothing else to do. I can tell you, Raymond and I have plenty to do with our time. We're just trying to help our neighbors."

I thought of my own neighbors. Jean and Jerry Flint live just west of me in a territorial-style home. Despite the high block fences separating houses on our street, occasionally we walk outside to our mailboxes at the same time and exchange a few friendly words.

To the east, Gloria and Ken Woodman have added Spanish archways and bay windows, giving their house a distinctive look. The Woodmans aren't home much, but we wave to each other whenever we happen to pull into or out of our driveways simultaneously.

Unlike Denise's neighbors, only Jean and Jerry walk around our street—and that's because they own an Irish setter. I don't often meet them because they walk Justinian in the early mornings and late evenings. Yet, even though we rarely socialize—both couples are busy with grown children and grandchildren—I know I can count on the Flints and Woodmans in an emergency. They were so good to me during Bob's last illness.

"They don't appreciate our help," Raymond was saying when I tuned back in. "They're all so afraid we'll gossip about them. I don't know what they have to hide."

Denise brought over dishes of chocolate-swirl ice cream with peanut-butter cookies on the side. It was now past ten P.M., and I accepted mine gratefully, remembering that I hadn't had anything to eat since lunch.

"I know you don't want to get involved with the police," Denise said to the Brandens, "but I'd like Ruthie's opinion about what happened Sunday night."

The Brandens looked at each other in surprise. I wondered why they thought Denise had asked all of us to her house at this late hour, if not to hear their story. They seemed in no hurry to speak; yet I could tell that Verna was bursting with her news.

"Denise said she told you about the big argument over there." Verna nodded toward the Stokes house.

"Just that Betsy rushed over here to get away from the others."

"Who knows what might have happened if Raymond and I weren't passing by? We kept them from following her into this house. I tell you the way Richard Stokes looked, I wouldn't be surprised if he tried to strangle me."

"I was right there, wasn't I?" Raymond asked.

"It was like a lynch mob," she continued without acknowledging him. "I never had much use for Betsy, marrying poor Harry for what she could get out of him. But four against one isn't right. She didn't know what to do, but I said, 'Just go on over to Denise's, and I'll take care of these bullies.'"

"Did they hurt her?"

"Not when they saw those big flashlights Raymond and I carry. I held mine up like a club. And they stood back, I can tell you."

"What did they say?"

"They didn't dare say another word. The son and his wife got into their Mercedes, and the daughter got on her boyfriend's motorcycle, and that was that."

"Betsy should have called the police," Raymond said.

"I wanted to call them, but she wouldn't let me," Denise told him. Their comments lacked the intensity I would have expected, which convinced me they had all been exchanged before.

"What were they arguing about?"

"She didn't want to talk," Denise said. "But Verna and Raymond heard enough to guess the rest."

"We were just making our rounds. About ten-thirty, it was. Most people are watching TV at that hour or asleep. We never hear conversations. And hardly ever arguments."

"These houses were built well," Raymond added.

I suspected if the Brandens missed anything that went on in the neighborhood, it wasn't because of negligence on their part. But unwilling to put ideas into their heads, I couldn't ask what I most wanted to know. Did they see Michael on Sunday night? Instead I listened to their story.

"They must have been in the front room because we could hear them shouting. I mean, we couldn't tell who it was or what was happening—it could have been a burglary in progress—so we went up the front walk to make sure everyone was okay."

Denise interrupted. "Did you know that Betsy's pregnant?"

I acknowledged that I knew and waited to hear more. Verna appeared to be gathering her strength by cramming one cookie after another into her mouth. I wondered how she stayed so thin.

"It was awful," she said. "Richard kept asking whose baby she's carrying. 'You killed Dad so he wouldn't find out the truth about the baby. I know it's not his.'

"'You're crazy,' Betsy shrieked at him.

"'If you think you can get away with this, you're the one who's crazy. We'll see to it that you don't get a cent of Dad's money.'"

"That was the first we heard about a baby," Raymond said.

Verna picked up the story again. "I was afraid for Betsy. Richard was accusing her of murder. But he sounded so violent, I'm sure he's really the one who did it."

"Anyways, I rang the doorbell," Raymond said, "but no one answered at first. Then Betsy called out to wait a minute. It all happened so fast; the daughter-in-law opened the door a crack, and Betsy pushed her aside and ran. That's when Verna and me kept them from following her."

"Where was her father when all that was going on?" I asked. Although Denise had already told me he wasn't around, I wanted to see if the Brandens would corroborate her information. I waited, wondering what they would say about Michael, afraid that Betsy had said something to implicate him in Joey's death.

"I asked her that first thing," Verna said. "She told me he had a dinner appointment and he never came back."

"Dinner appointment," Denise said. "I thought he was in Tucson."

"Maybe the dinner date was in Tucson," I said, but this new discrepancy between Michael's account of his whereabouts and Betsy's words when she was at her most distraught hit me like a blow to the head.

Eighteen

On my drive home that night, I decided to see Michael as soon as possible. I would not rely on Betsy's neighbors for information but would approach him directly. Clearly her neighbors suspected Richard Stokes, and I wanted to believe they were right. But although I hated to doubt Michael, I had to know why he lied about Sunday evening. Since I was on the late shift the next day, I decided to call him in the morning.

I didn't sleep well again that night. Vivid pictures of the Stokes family chasing Betsy flashed through my mind. Even though I knew her pregnancy wasn't that far advanced, I saw her as big as if she were at term, clumsily running from the others. Only in my dream, Michael was one of those chasing her.

Immediately after breakfast I telephoned. Betsy answered. "It's Ruth Morris," I said. "Is your dad there?"

"He went out for a while, but I expect him back soon. Would you like to come over and wait for him?"

I was surprised at the invitation but decided to take advantage of it. Maybe Betsy didn't want to be alone in the house after the events of Sunday night.

When I pulled into their driveway, I saw Michael's silver-and-gray Lexus through the open garage door. This encounter would be awkward no matter what happened, but I was relieved not to have to make small talk with Betsy.

He opened the door for me and I followed him into the entryway, past the two white fluted columns, and stepped down into Betsy's living room, all sharp angles in black and white. It looked different today without the crowd who'd filled the house after the funeral.

I had dressed carefully in an off-white pleated skirt with a black and white blouse. If my blouse had been a geometric rather than a paisley print, I'd have fit right into the room. Michael, wearing white tennis shorts and a navy pullover, looked bright and cheerful, if a bit flushed. I wondered if he'd been out playing tennis despite the heat.

He led me to one of the black wrought-iron armchairs, which I would have mistaken for outdoor furniture if not for their overstuffed white cushions. I sat down but Michael remained standing. He had picked up a small terra-cotta coyote from the lamp table next to me and was turning it round and round in his hands. I thought of the stone coyotes circling the fountain where Joey died. But this was foolish. I knew well enough that coyotes were popular in southwestern art now and, in fact, could see them pictured in an oil painting over the sofa and an alabaster sculpture in front of the windows. It was probably Betsy's way, or an interior decorator's way, of reconciling the southwestern exterior of the house and its sleek, ultramodern indoor look. Watching Michael, I wondered if he also associated the coyotes with Joey's death.

"Are you off today or are you on nights?" he asked.

"Nights." One advantage of being with other pharmacists is not having to explain our odd work schedules.

"I'm glad you stopped by, Ruthie."

Realizing this was his polite way of finding out why I wanted to see him, I plunged in. "I'm worried. Betsy's neighbors told me what happened here Sunday night, and I think it may be connected with the two deaths."

"I'm sure my daughter appreciates your concern," he said drily, a touch of coldness in his tone.

This was not going as I'd anticipated. "It's you I'm worried about right now, not Betsy," I blurted.

"Let me get this straight. You're worried about me because Harry's children are being nasty to my daughter."

His words did make me sound ridiculous, but I would not be sidetracked. "You know what I mean. Twice now you've said you intend to act as bait to trap the murderer. Have you considered that those accusations by Richard and the others may be smoke screens to hide their own complicity?"

"Yes, and that's exactly what I had in mind when I revved up my campaign."

"But it's dangerous."

"It's more dangerous to have a murderer on the loose."

We had both raised our voices, and Betsy now appeared in the doorway between living and dining rooms. I was surprised to see her in an off-white maternity dress with red-and-black vertical stripes. Surely she was in the third month at most. But maybe this was her way of announcing the pregnancy to friends, family, and nosy neighbors. I wondered whether Betsy had worn maternity clothes Sunday night, and if that had precipitated the quarrel with Harry's children.

"Will you have some cold juice?" She was carrying two glasses filled with crushed ice and orange juice, and held one out to each of us.

"What about you, hon?" Michael asked her.

"I had some while you were at the tennis courts."

"You may as well join us instead of wondering what we're talking about." Michael's voice had softened as he spoke to his daughter.

She walked over and took the coyote figure out of

his hands. "Look at you," she said. "And you keep telling me to be calm."

"I'm not the pregnant one."

"You could have fooled me." She was flippant with her father, but I saw that she was concerned about him, too. I didn't know how frank I should be about Sunday night with Betsy in the room, but after a moment she turned to me.

"My neighbors used to annoy me. I thought they were always prying, so mostly I tried to avoid them. But the other night, I found out how much it means to have good neighbors."

"Denise really is a caring person," I said.

"I know that now."

"You have to admit she can be intrusive at times," Michael added. "She's been over here just about every day."

"When Harry was alive, she only came by when he was home. I used to think she had a crush on him. But I guess I was wrong."

I sipped my orange juice and said nothing. Denise must have been pretty obvious.

"For a while, I suspected her of somehow causing Harry's death. But Sunday night, she was so good to me that I changed my mind. Now after that young man's murder, I don't know what to think. Especially since he worked at Food Go with Denise."

Like carousel riders, suspicion kept spinning round and round. No wonder the police seemed to be baffled. I decided this wasn't the right time to remind Betsy that Joey had worked in *my* department at Food Go.

"What happened Sunday night?" I asked since she had brought up the subject.

Betsy looked embarrassed and I doubted she'd tell me anything. But I was wrong. "It was very unpleasant," she began and hesitated.

"You may as well tell Ruthie the details before she gets a distorted story from someone else," Michael said. He was still standing, twirling the juice glass in his hands now.

"Harry's children have always been cold to me, but they didn't dare confront me while he was alive. They mostly talked to him and ignored me."

Michael's expression had hardened. "I warned you that would happen if you married a man with grown children."

"Yes, Dad. And you didn't want me to marry Tim Barnard before Harry, and you had something against everyone else I ever went out with."

That was interesting news. I wondered whether I should add Tim to my list of suspects, but all the vengeful ex-husbands and boyfriends I'd ever read about went after the woman who threw them over. Sometimes they killed the men who supplanted them, too, but surely Betsy would have been the primary target. And, I thought, he wouldn't have waited all this time either.

Michael hadn't answered his daughter. She paused a moment and continued. "After . . . afterward, Dad was here, so they couldn't say too much. They managed to get some digs in. Mostly Richard. I think the others might have accepted me if he weren't so . . . so negative."

"You've probably heard gossip that Harry was a rich man," Michael said. "Well, the nosy neighbors were right this time; he was quite successful in real estate and the stock market. But Betsy would have been better off if he hadn't done so well financially. It's the money that keeps his children steamed up."

"They all think I married him for it. Couldn't they recognize his zest for life? Couldn't they see how attractive it made him? Age doesn't change that." Her voice lowered as she tried to control her emotions.

Her words made me think again of Yeats's poem, and I could understand Betsy. It wasn't only Michael whose compelling personality could not be diminished by age.

"Anyhow, Dad had to go to Tucson for the weekend." Did I imagine that she hesitated over the name of the city? I certainly didn't imagine the way she shifted in her chair or the way Michael's eyes would not meet mine.

"I don't know how they found out I was alone here. Maybe they came by and didn't see Dad's car in the driveway."

"Maybe one of your wonderful neighbors called them," Michael said sarcastically.

She ignored the remark. "When they all arrived at the same time, I knew it was prearranged. I guess I was foolish to let them in, but they *are* Harry's family.

"Richard wanted me to divide everything equally between him and Sheila—she's his sister—and sign it all over to them. He said he'd 'let me' keep the house if I did that.

"I reminded them that Harry had changed the beneficiaries of his Living Trust because they were into him for so much money. He told me he was tired of supporting his grown children.

"Richard started shouting at me. It was dreadful—"

"Okay, hon, it's over," Michael interrupted. "They won't bother you while I'm here."

"And what happens later?"

"We get a restraining order if they won't stay away from you."

Betsy turned toward me again. "It got worse. Richard said if I didn't sign over everything, he'd go to the police. He said he had proof that I killed Harry."

"What kind of proof?"

"He said Harry died because I gave him my medicine, and he knew it was deliberate."

"You should know that he accused me, too," I told her.

"And me," Michael said.

"You've told me that before, Dad, but it's not the same. They always suspect the spouse. And all of them—Richard and his wife and Sheila and Scott—each one said they'd testify that Harry and I fought constantly."

I remembered Michael's words about the quarrels over the expected baby, but couldn't bring up that subject unless one of them did first. "Many husbands and wives argue, but that doesn't mean they murder each other," I said.

"Yes, but they did find my Food-Fed on Harry's night table."

"And the police have known that from the beginning," Michael reassured her. It sounded like something he'd told her before. "There's nothing Harry's children can do to harm you."

"The situation has changed now," I said. "If you have an alibi for the time that Joey died—"

"Unless it happened earlier than what they're saying on the news, I don't have one."

"It's a shame your Dad was gone that night," I said. I avoided looking at Michael, but I could hear him move toward the armchair next to mine and heard the chair shift as he sat down.

"You ought to tell her," Betsy said.

"Yes, I was just about to." Michael rose and began to pace again. "The police already know I was here Sunday night. I had dinner with Joey."

"I know. Joey's parents told me."

His eyes held mine as if he were trying to reach beyond them into my thoughts. "So you're here because you suspected me, not because you're concerned about me."

I tried to ignore the cold tone that had returned to his voice. "Wouldn't you be suspicious of me if you discovered I lied to you?"

"No, Ruthie. If I didn't trust you, I'd be probing to find out whether you gave Harry something that wasn't prescribed for him. After all, you were his pharmacist."

"You think I . . ." My voice trailed off in disbelief.

"That's not what I said. *I* trust *you*."

Now I was angry enough to shout at him. "I'm not the one who claimed to be in Tucson when Joey was killed. And all the time you were with him."

"I wasn't with him."

"Make up your mind." I was still shouting.

"It looks like you've made up yours." His voice was icy now.

Betsy intervened. "Calm down both of you. You're acting like children."

"I'm sorry," I said. "I'm not myself today."

"We've all been upset the last few weeks. Let's start over." He moved his chair closer to mine. "Joey and I met at the Sizzler at seven-thirty Sunday night. We were there, eating and talking, for about an hour and a half. Then he went off, and I hurried back to Tucson."

"You drove to Scottsdale and back to Tucson just to have dinner with Joey?" I couldn't keep the skepticism from my voice.

"You really don't trust me," Michael said.

"What would you think if someone told you that? Supposing Richard or Denise kept changing stories?"

"It would depend on what I thought of that person to begin with."

"I see," I said. "I'm supposed to take it on faith because we knew each other all those years ago."

"No," Betsy said. "You don't have to take it on faith. I was there, too."

Nineteen

Michael's face paled as he turned to his daughter. "We agreed never to tell anyone."

"What's the use, Dad? When the police check your story, someone will remember seeing me there."

"No one will remember. That's why Joey picked the Sizzler in the first place."

I looked from one to another, not knowing whether this development exonerated both father and daughter or implicated them further. "Would one of you tell me what's going on?"

"First of all," Betsy said, "let me assure you that Dad really did go to Tucson on Saturday night, and he intended to return here late on Monday."

"I had doubts about leaving Betsy alone, but she said she wanted to get used to it gradually."

A spontaneous spasm of pity gripped me and, for the first time, I felt more than superficial identification with Betsy. I remembered the indescribable loneliness of those first weeks and months of widowhood, and I wanted to comfort her. Now I understood that trip to the toy store. If buying a stuffed elephant for the expected baby provided a few moments of solace, Denise and I were wrong to criticize.

"If only I hadn't told him about Joey's call when Dad phoned Sunday morning to see how I was doing," Betsy said.

"Joey called you?"

"He said he had something to tell my father."

"But who suggested dinner? Joey was comfortable talking to people, but I can't see him inviting Michael to dinner at the Sizzler."

"Why not?" Michael asked.

"For one thing, he didn't know you." I said lamely.

Betsy laughed. It was a musical laugh with an underlying sweetness that destroyed once and for all the golddigger image implanted by Denise. I knew I was foolish to judge her by that sound and the brief change in her expression. But I suddenly thought that Betsy could have been my daughter, mine and Michael's. Fighting a sadness that threatened to overwhelm me, I asked as calmly as I could, "Did the two of you know the Franklins socially?"

The musical laugh was softer this time. "That's a tactful way to phrase the question. No, I didn't even realize who he was when he phoned." Her face became serious now. "When he said he was the pharmacy technician, I thought he meant at the hospital down in Tucson. I was terrified that something had happened to Dad."

Ashamed of my suspicions, I decided to listen without comment. Surely Betsy would not be telling all this to me if she or Michael had anything to do with Joey's death. It seemed absurd to link either of them to the murder. Yet someone had killed Joey, and because of the Stokes connection, the chances were that I knew the person. I could not eliminate Betsy or Michael or Denise from suspicion just because I liked them.

"Joey said he wanted to meet my father at seven-thirty Sunday night, and he repeated that he had something very important to tell Dad, and only him."

But Michael was already in Tucson, I thought, and nearly interrupted to ask why Betsy hadn't postponed the dinner appointment until his return. Betsy answered my unspoken question.

"I was afraid to tell Joey that Dad was away, so I

said I'd give him the message. Actually I was going to meet Joey instead."

"Then I called and hit the ceiling when I heard about it."

I was outraged. "Surely Joey wasn't one of your suspects, Michael."

"You have to understand that I didn't really know Joey. At that point, I suspected everyone until I could logically eliminate them."

"Joey was eliminated all right," I said bitterly. "Do we all have to be killed before we get off your list?"

"And what about your list?"

"Truce," I said. "I promise to listen quietly from now on."

Betsy continued. "I refused to break the appointment, so Dad insisted on joining us."

"Tucson is not in outer space," Michael said. "It took less than two hours to race back up here."

"Dad told me he'd meet us at the restaurant, and I shouldn't leave before he turned up no matter what happened."

This reminded me of those suspense novels where the murder suspect gets the heroine to rendezvous in some dark, forbidding place without letting anyone else know. But in this case, the person who was killed was the one who arranged the meeting. If Betsy and Michael were telling the truth, I reminded myself. Their story sounded plausible so far; I would try to reserve judgment until I heard it all.

"The truth—and we are telling you the truth, Ruthie—is that I wanted to give them a chance to sit down and start eating before I appeared. Betsy was going to assure him that I'd be there any minute."

"What did Joey say?"

"That's the problem," Michael said. "He dropped hints, but he didn't reveal much."

"He told me Detective Moreway was his brother-in-law, so he knew all about the case. That's what he called Harry's death—the case." Betsy's voice was tightly controlled. I guessed from the quick glance she gave her father that she was more concerned about worrying him than breaking down in front of me.

"Joey was only twenty years old," I said. "To him, the drama and mystery overshadowed the human beings whose lives were touched."

"A nice enough young man, but at that age they think everyone over thirty is too old to feel anything," Michael said drily.

"I know you've heard all this already, Dad, but let me tell it to Ruthie from the beginning. Since she knew Joey so much better than we did, maybe she can figure out what was behind it all.

"Joey was in cutoffs and a T-shirt, but so were half the people in the restaurant. We went up to the salad bar first, and he filled his plate with spaghetti and meat sauce. No salad. I tried to make a joke about it, asking didn't his mom ever tell him salads are healthy. He was very polite, but I could see he didn't appreciate the remark.

"Joey said he wanted to talk to Dad first and then his brother-in-law. He explained that if he told everything to Detective Moreway, he was afraid it would become part of the official record. He didn't want to get anyone in trouble, but something was bothering him.

"Then he began a long explanation about how helpful Denise had always been to him. I guessed the two ideas were connected, and it was Denise he was afraid of hurting.

"He asked whether I knew that Denise had wanted my husband to finance her education. Actually I'd never heard that, but I tried to be noncommittal. I was embarrassed to have him think Harry kept things from me."

"Denise told me all about it," I said, figuring there was no longer any reason to keep quiet. It could be important to emphasize that Denise herself had told me, that it was not a secret. I didn't like what I was hearing, and I wanted to balance the scales. "It wasn't the way it sounds. Denise wants to become a dental technician; she would have drawn up a promissory note and started paying him back as soon as she got a job."

"She had a job," Michael said in that cold voice that made me so uncomfortable.

"Everyone has dreams," I said. "Maybe Denise had unrealistic ones, but I don't believe she'd ever harm anyone."

"Joey said she was furious when Harry turned her down."

"Are you trying to say that Joey implicated Denise?" I felt queasy, almost as sick as when I first heard from the Franklins about Joey's dinner appointment with Michael. "Let's be logical about it. Why would she kill Joey if he'd already told *you* what he knew about Harry's death?"

"That's the problem," Michael said. "He didn't reveal what he knew. When I joined them that night, my daughter insisted on hearing what he had to tell me, and Joey wouldn't say another word."

"Did you ask Denise about it?" I turned to Betsy, hoping for a negative response.

"Yes," she said, looking miserable. "The same night. The night Joey was murdered."

"What are you talking about? Denise didn't know anything about his death until Monday afternoon." She couldn't be that good an actress, I thought.

"Don't you see the point we're making?" Michael asked. "We were in the Sizzler with Joey until about nine o'clock. Since Betsy and I'd come in separate cars, she drove home from the restaurant and I rushed right back to Tucson."

"Dad wanted to follow me home to make sure I got there safely. But I told him I'm a big girl now." She smiled at her father.

"And then Harry's children came here that night and started playing their little games with Betsy.

When the neighbors, and that includes Denise, tried to help her, it must have been close to eleven."

I didn't want them to know the Brandens had already told me it was 10:30. And who knows? That nosy couple could have been outside this house listening to the argument for some time.

"Denise and I talked for a while. I told her everything Joey had said, as tactfully as I could. She seemed embarrassed, but was very kind and walked me back to my front door to make sure the others hadn't returned."

"And that must have been around midnight," Michael said.

I knew what he was implying. According to the TV and newspapers, Joey had been killed between midnight and 5:30 in the morning. Reporters had gotten to the man who'd been on duty at the guard gate that night. In response to their questions, he said he'd walked past the fountain just before his shift began at midnight. "Everything looked the same as always," he said. "The fountain was still lit up—it's on a timer— and I could see it was okay."

During the summer, like many people who had to work outdoors in the Arizona heat, the groundskeepers for the complex began work at 5:30. Probably the medical examiner could narrow the time, but I no longer had a pipeline to information from Frank Moreway. Poor Joey, I thought. I wonder if those insider details he got from his brother-in-law somehow led to his death.

The timing didn't eliminate anybody. If Michael really had left for Tucson at nine, he wasn't a suspect, but we had only his word for it unless someone in that city corroborated his story. A painful possibility leaped into my mind. Was Michael living with someone in Tucson? Would she vouch for his arrival there and give him an alibi for the early morning hours that followed? I certainly couldn't ask Michael, but the police probably had already done so.

In the old days, Michael's deep blue eyes had often seemed to penetrate my thoughts. He hadn't lost the knack. "If you're wondering whether anyone saw me in Tucson that night," he said, "no such luck. So if you're still suspicious of me, I have no alibi until the next morning when I popped into the hospital pharmacy where I work. And, of course, that doesn't mean anything. I could have driven there directly from Scottsdale that morning instead of spending the night at my home in Tucson."

I found I was more interested in the fact that he lived alone than in the lack of corroboration for his story. This won't do, I told myself, and was about to try to find out the details of Michael's interrogation when the doorbell rang. Betsy went to answer it. I half expected to see Denise follow her into the living room, but the newcomers were Sheila Stokes and her fiancé, Scott Robbins.

Sheila was wearing the SCOTTY'S GROUPIE T-shirt again, but the letters were an iridescent green this time. I wondered if she had a whole wardrobe of shirts proclaiming her status as Scott's girlfriend.

Michael was on his feet, a torrent of angry words beginning to erupt, but Betsy took his arm and quieted him with a look. "Dad, Sheila and Scott came to apologize for Sunday night."

"That's right," Sheila said. "We didn't want you to think we agreed with Richard."

"It took you long enough to decide. Why didn't you support Betsy when she needed you?"

Sheila stood in the middle of the living room, looking awkwardly from Betsy to Michael. No one had invited her to sit down and, considering that she must have grown up in this house, I thought it an unfortunate oversight. "I've known since childhood it's no use reasoning with my brother when he's in that kind of mood."

"And he ignores *me*," Scott added without a trace of embarrassment. He was wearing black bicycle shorts that left nothing to the imagination and a Hard Rock Cafe T-shirt. "He won't even give me credit for trying to better myself. Why does he think I'm over there in Tempe every day, taking classes at the University?"

"I told you not to take it personally, Scotty," Sheila said. Their exchange reverberated with the echo of countless repetitions. I didn't want to miss the confrontation that was about to take place, but felt I had to be polite. As I was the only one still seated, I got up and mumbled something about leaving.

"You sit right down, Ruthie," Michael said loudly. "You're the only one who was invited here."

"Dad!"

"I'm tired of being courteous to people who've treated my daughter shabbily from day one."

Sheila looked as if she'd been slapped. "I didn't mean to be rotten to Betsy. It was the shock of Dad getting married again. And to someone so young."

"You're trying to tell me that an older stepmother would have been all right. Don't make me laugh! It's been the money all along."

"He was my father," Sheila said.

"And I'm Betsy's father, and no one is going to hurt her again."

"Now just a minute," Scott said. "Sheila is not out to hurt anyone. She cares about people, not money."

"You think we don't know how much Harry gave his children. A hundred and fifty thousand to each of you over the last few years, and still you and Richard always had your hands out for more."

"Richard thinks we deserve what's in the trust. I'm sure my father didn't want to cut us out. Why, there's more than a million."

"And a good part of that is tied up in this house. You're not going to get your hands on it. Betsy and the baby need a place to live."

"Dad, please." Betsy was tugging Michael's arm, trying to get him away from Sheila and Scott.

Sheila looked as if she were ready to cry. "You heard what Richard said. We wouldn't touch the house. It's the rest of the money."

"Oh, yes, you want my daughter to turn everything but the house over to you."

"That's what Richard wants. I think we should divide it three ways."

"How generous of you," Michael said, and I could hear the sarcasm in his voice.

"Hey, man, there's enough for everyone," Scott said.

"Evidently a hundred and fifty thousand dollars wasn't enough for Sheila or Richard."

"Money goes fast when you're out of a job; my brother has to have enough to tide him over until he finds something else. If Betsy would only be fair, Richard might even be able to start his own business."

"Just like me," Scott said.

"Look, Scott, I remember you from Tucson. You've never kept a job for more than two or three months."

"And I remember you from Tucson, too. I remember how you talked your daughter out of seeing me, and how you objected to Tim and everyone else she ever dated. You always treated her like a princess. No one was good enough for Betsy Loring."

He turned to Sheila. "You know what, I'm going to talk to that cop about him. He probably killed your father so his own daughter would get all the money."

Twenty

Round and round we go, I thought. I wanted badly to step off this merry-go-round, but it was my own fault for getting so involved. I waited to hear Michael's reaction to the accusation, but he said nothing. Instead he walked past the white fluted columns and into the small entryway. A rush of hot air mingled with the artificially cooled atmosphere of the house. I knew he'd opened the front door even though I couldn't see it from where I'd just reseated myself.

Sheila looked toward the door and then at Scott. He shrugged his shoulders in a gesture of noninvolvement. "I'm sorry," she said to Betsy, and the two of them left the house. A moment later, I heard Scott's motorcycle start up. I couldn't tell if he were gunning the engine in defiance or if that was how he always drove, but the noise faded and Michael returned to the living room.

"Well, now you know what it's been like for Betsy," he said to me.

"Everyone's accusing everyone else. That won't catch the murderer."

"The police questioned me for more than three hours yesterday." Michael sighed heavily and sat down again. "If they had evidence against anyone at all, I don't think they would have wasted so much time on me."

"Maybe they don't consider it wasted time." I could have bitten my tongue for saying that.

Michael considered me impassively. "You still don't trust me."

"That's not the point. What happens when they find out you lied?"

"Are you going to tell them?"

I wanted to cry out that I wouldn't be the one to turn him in even if he'd killed Joey, but I just shook my head. "I suppose Detective Moreway will question me again," I said.

"You have no first-hand information about Sunday night," Michael told me. "Only hearsay, and that's not evidence."

Now he was throwing legalisms at me. I wondered how long it would be before he hired an attorney for himself and Betsy. Ironically, I'd come there to find out what really happened Sunday night so I could stop suspecting Michael. Instead, when I left the Stokes house and got back into my car, I was no closer to the truth and still suspicious of him.

At home, I slathered mustard on two slices of rye bread and sliced some salami to go with it. I didn't feel up to lunch in the coffee shop, where I'd have to talk to Denise. There was nothing about this morning's visit that I wanted to discuss with her, so I was careful to clock in and go straight to the pharmacy. Detective Frank Moreway, neatly dressed in a white shirt, red-figured power tie, and lightweight blue pants, the fabric of which looked like seersucker but wasn't, was waiting for me. I looked quickly at his shoes to see whether they were black or brown. Brown would mean that he was not infallible.

"I tried to see you at home this morning," he said.

"I was out."

"So I discovered. Where can we talk?"

Tim's and my shifts overlapped on Wednesdays, so the pharmacy was covered. I turned around and walked over to the employee lounge with Frank

Moreway, hoping we could find a quiet corner. One of the bakery clerks was on break, reading a movie magazine, but she didn't even look up when we entered the lounge. We sat as far across the room as we could get from her. When he crossed his legs, I saw that he was wearing navy blue socks and brown shoes. He was not infallible after all.

"The other pharmacist told me when to expect you." He looked around. "I wanted to talk to you privately."

"Then it's either after nine-thirty tonight or about five tomorrow afternoon."

"Yes, he said you're on early tomorrow. Tell me, how do the shifts work? I thought you worked one late week and one early week, but now I see that doesn't necessarily follow."

Why did I feel so nervous around this man? He was doing his job, and I should be glad to help him track down Joey's killer. I studied his face. He had dark circles under his eyes and seemed different from the self-confident policeman who'd questioned me before. I wondered if he could be objective about the case now that his brother-in-law was a victim, and why they hadn't put someone else on it.

A produce clerk and one of the meat cutters walked into the room, and Frank Moreway must have realized a private conversation was now impossible, especially when the meat cutter took a seat at our table.

"Is this cop pestering you, Ruthie?" he asked.

"No," I said. "Not at all."

"Well, we want you to catch the turkey who did Joey in," he said to Detective Moreway. "But if you're going to waste time questioning my favorite pharmacist here, you'll never find him."

Frank Moreway looked annoyed at the interruption, but told him politely that this was just routine. He waited awhile, evidently trying to decide whether to continue despite the lack of privacy. After some minutes in thought, he asked me more about my working hours. "I take it you have a definite schedule. It doesn't just change from day to night to day randomly."

"No, of course not. We have to be able to plan things if we want to go out with friends or go to plays or ballgames or whatever."

"So, how does it work?"

"Basically, it's a two-week schedule, with every other weekend off. I have it posted in the pharmacy, if you want to see it."

"That's retail for you," the meat cutter said. "Terrible hours."

Frank Moreway ignored him. "Were you off this past Sunday?"

Until that question, I hadn't realized what he was leading up to. I looked straight at him. "Detective," I said, "why don't you just ask me where I was that night. It doesn't matter what my schedule is here because the pharmacy closes at six o'clock on Sundays. I worked from opening to closing and then went home, so I have no alibi."

"And how did you know what time you need the alibi for?"

"Give her a break," the meat cutter said. "We all saw it on TV."

Now Frank Moreway turned to him. I could see he was holding in his anger, whether because of the interruptions and lack of privacy or because television news had interfered with his job, I didn't know. "Don't believe everything you see on TV," was all he said.

The meat cutter winked at me and got up. "Break's over. Gotta go."

"What was the time of death?" I asked.

"Just what you heard. Between midnight and five-thirty in the morning."

"Then why are you wasting time asking about my work schedule? Are you trying to intimidate me that way?"

"I told you, this is routine questioning. Anyhow,

Food Go is open twenty-four hours a day. I didn't know the pharmacy hours were different."

"They're posted."

"Yes, I suppose they are." He looked so unhappy, I suddenly regretted arguing with him. After all, if I hadn't been worried about implicating my friends, I would have cooperated fully. I decided to do so unless the questions veered toward them.

"I'm sorry," I said. "It's been a strain for all of us, but I'm sure it's worse for you. Ask me whatever you'd like."

"You worked with Joey for a long time, and I know he had only good things to say about you. I need to know if he said anything at all these last few weeks that seemed odd."

"Odd," I echoed.

"Let's say out of character, unusual, surprising. Anything at all that I should know."

"I've been trying to think along those lines, too, but I haven't found anything. His folks told me he'd been different since the Stokes funeral, but I never noticed."

"Yes, the Stokes funeral. Why did Joey attend?"

"I don't know."

"He went with you and Mrs. Seaford?"

"That's right."

"Tell me how that happened."

I tried to remember the funeral. It was only nine days ago, but it seemed like a month or more had passed. Joey had invited himself a few days beforehand. Although I didn't want to reveal Denise's plea that I go with her, I told Frank Moreway she had offered to do the driving and Joey had asked to join us.

"And where did she pick him up, at Food Go or at his home?"

Uh-oh. I was on the merry-go-round again, and Frank Moreway was searching for the one who had the brass ring. I decided this was too easy to check and told the truth.

"So you were both familiar with the complex. And you couldn't have helped seeing the fountain when you drove in."

"Just a minute," I said. "Thousands of people must have seen the fountain. What are you trying to do?"

"Just routine," he insisted again. "Why are you so upset?"

"I'm not upset."

"Then why are you raising your voice?"

"You're making me sound like a suspect. First you questioned my work schedule, and now you're asking if I'm familiar with the place where Joey died."

"I told you, this is routine. We're asking the same questions of everyone who knew Joey or worked with him. And we're also going back to those who knew Harry Stokes."

"So you have connected the two deaths," I said.

"Not officially, but we can't rule out a relationship. I take it from your comment that you see a connection?" His tone alerted me that this was a question, and as he waited pointedly, I knew he expected a response from me.

"Coincidences do happen, but I thought all along there was something strange about Harry Stokes's death. And together with what your in-laws said about Joey's behavior since then . . ."

"That's too vague. Do you have any concrete reason to suspect the Stokes death wasn't from natural causes?"

When I admitted that I had only vague suspicions, he was silent for a minute, staring at the door to the employee lounge. I twisted in my seat to find out the reason and saw that Denise had walked into the room. She was wearing her green Food Go apron with the patch pockets over an electric blue skirt. Her blouse was green, too. The colors should have clashed, but on Denise they looked interesting.

She sent one startled look our way, seemed to be on the verge of rushing off, hesitated, and came over to our table. "Have you found Joey's murderer yet?" she asked.

"We're working on it."

"Well, you won't find anything here. You need to check out all of Harry Stokes's family, including the ones related by marriage."

"What makes you say that?" he asked her.

"Isn't it obvious?"

"Maybe it's not to me. Why don't you sit down and explain what you mean?"

Denise took the seat across the table from Detective Moreway and proceeded to tell him all about the quarrel at the Stokes house Sunday evening. I was sure he'd had all the details from Michael on Tuesday, but I kept quiet. I was hearing the story for the third time, and I wondered if it would be exactly the same. Although I thought Denise was dramatizing the details for Frank Moreway's benefit, her basic story hadn't changed.

"And what did you do after Betsy Stokes returned to her own house?"

"After all that commotion, I was exhausted. I went right to sleep, Detective," she said.

I couldn't figure Denise out. When she discussed the situation with me, she seemed to relish her role as a possible suspect. But now she had opened her eyes wide in a parody of innocence. Maybe Frank Moreway didn't know her well enough to recognize that this pose wasn't Denise's normal look, but I did. It was as though she were playing a game with me or with the police.

Detective Moreway stood. "Thank you both for your cooperation," he said. "And Mrs. Morris, will you do me a favor and send the other pharmacist over here for a few minutes? I'm sure you can spare Tim once you're back on duty."

Denise left with me, although I knew she hadn't used up her break time. "What do you think?" she asked as soon as we were out of the room.

"I think he has no hard evidence at this point."

"That's not what I mean. Does he suspect me?"

I realized for the first time how self-centered Denise could be. Usually this aspect of her character was hidden beneath her concern for others, but now I wondered which was the real Denise. And how far would that person go to get what she wanted. "You see that he's talking to everyone. If you hadn't walked in, he wouldn't have asked you those questions."

"He would have come after me next. After Tim, anyhow." She lowered her voice. "Why Tim? He hardly knew Harry Stokes."

I remembered some of the comments Scott had made, remarks to which I hadn't paid much attention. "It seems to be routine, but it may be because Tim knew the family down in Tucson."

"Be serious," Denise said. "Tim may have a negative personality, but murder two people?"

"I'm beginning to think we can't rule out anyone," I told her.

"You suspect me, too. I know you do."

"Denise, please." We had just reached the pharmacy and several people were waiting at the window. I excused myself, gave Tim the message, and took over at the computer.

Greg Blackstone, the store manager, had promised me some help from other departments until we could find and train a new technician, but so far no one had materialized. I filled the prescription Tim had been working on, handed it over to the young woman who was waiting, and braced myself for a busy afternoon. I recognized the other two people at the window, a middle-aged woman and her elderly mother, although I didn't remember their names.

"I need a refill, but I don't have the prescription number," the daughter said timidly. "Is it okay?"

"No problem," I assured her, even though it meant more work for me. "What was the prescription for?"

"Thank you so much," she said. "It's for those nicotine patches. Now that Mother is with us, I'm worried about her emphysema. I've just got to stop smoking."

What a pleasure to help an appreciative customer, I thought, as I asked her name and looked the record up in the computer. I refilled her Nicoderm and handed it over, to a chorus of thanks from daughter and mother.

For the next half hour, I was too busy to worry about Harry Stokes and Joey Franklin, but when Tim returned looking sullen, I tried to find out about his interview without overt prying. He was unforthcoming at the best of times, and I tried to be tactful.

"Detective Moreway doesn't seem to have anything definite," I said. "I think he's on a fishing expedition."

Tim just grunted and busied himself at the computer, leaving the telephones and the window to me as usual. Knowing I would have to be more direct, I tried again at the first lull. "Someone told me you used to date Betsy Stokes."

He compressed his lips into a thin line and was quiet for so long, I thought he wasn't going to respond. "It's no secret," he said finally.

"I suppose not. Scott Robbins seems to know all about it. He seemed to think her father caused the breakup." I was guessing here, because Scott could have been exaggerating. "That surprised me. After all, she's not a teenager."

"She's thirty-one. Same as me."

I persisted, knowing I had no right to ask. "And both of you were willing to listen to her father?"

"That shows how much you know," Tim said. "We went on seeing each other long after that phony intellectual tried to interfere."

Twenty-one

I looked at Tim, trying not to show my astonishment at his outburst. "And then what happened?" I dared to ask, holding my breath.

"You want to know what happened?" he asked in a loud voice. I glanced nervously at the window, but no one was in sight. "She loved me; she always loved me. But when she had the chance to marry money, she couldn't resist."

"You make a decent salary."

He laughed, but it wasn't a pleasant laugh. "Decent, sure. The same as her Dad. Well, Betsy grew up in a middle-class home, on a pharmacist's income, and she wanted more." His voice took on an earnest tone, as if he wanted to convince both of us. "You know how pretty she is; she deserved more, and I didn't begrudge it to her. I wanted her to have a beautiful house and nice things, so I didn't stand in her way when she married that old man."

Not so old, I automatically said to myself. But there were more important things to think about. Could Tim have killed Harry Stokes for revenge?

"I can see exactly what you're thinking," he said to me. "And it's stupid. If I wanted to get rid of that old guy, why would I have waited so long? I told you. I knew she married him for the beautiful home and all the other things he could give her, and I agreed."

"You agreed? I don't understand."

"If you must know, Betsy moved up here a few months before I transferred to Scottsdale. She used to come into the pharmacy here and tell me all about him. All the things he could do for her. It was a marriage of convenience."

What an old-fashioned phrase for someone of Tim's generation to use, I thought. Whether or not he realized it, he was echoing the slanders of Harry's children, and I no longer believed them.

"Marriage of convenience," I said before I had time to consider the implications. "Not when Betsy is pregnant." But he knows that, I realized as I spoke. His initials had been on the computer printout as the one who filled her prescription for Stuartnatal 1 + 1, the prenatal vitamins.

To my dismay, I saw Tim's face redden and braced myself for another outburst. But he turned away, took off his white jacket, carefully hung it up, and abruptly walked out of the pharmacy. It wasn't the first time he'd left for the day without saying anything, but I couldn't shake my uneasiness all afternoon and evening. I wondered whether Frank Moreway was aware of the relationship between Tim and Betsy. When I get home tonight, I'm going to think this through and decide whether it's important enough to tell the police, I promised myself.

Just before closing, I had a prescription for Retin-A, 0.01%. We were out of that strength, so I called some of the other Food Go stores and then two or three of our competitors. "No one has that strength in stock," I told the customer. "But I can catch tonight's order and have it here tomorrow."

"My son needs it to clear up his acne," she said. "I can't wait for you to order it."

"Then, I'll be happy to return the prescription," I told her. "You can try other pharmacies on your own, but you heard me check around."

"What will I do? It's an emergency."

Terminal acne, we called it among ourselves. We

were always surprised how unconcerned some people were with drugs like penicillin that they really needed immediately and how upset they could become if we were out of acne medicine. After thinking it over, the customer left the prescription to be picked up the next day, but I was twenty minutes late closing up.

I was half afraid to see Tim lurking in the parking lot and clutched my Mace canister tightly, but it was Denise who waited for me outside the main exit. She was still wearing the green blouse she'd had on earlier but had changed her skirt to a pair of white shorts. "What are you doing here?" I asked. "I thought you were on days."

"I came back to see you."

"Shall we go inside?"

"No, not here. The Village Inn on Indian School is open late. Will you meet me there?"

I sighed inwardly, but she seemed so desperate; I couldn't refuse her. During the ten-minute drive to the restaurant, I anticipated another dramatic encounter. Funny, I thought, none of the detective stories I've read reveal how exhausting it is to be in the middle of a murder mystery.

Denise was waiting just inside the entrance to the Village Inn. Only two tables were occupied in the nonsmoking section, and the hostess tried to seat us between them. "No, we want to be over there," Denise told her and pointed to a booth at the opposite end of the place.

"Why do restaurants always try to put everyone in one area?" I asked after we were seated.

"That's because it's easier for the help. You'd be surprised, though, how many people won't take the table I want to give them in the coffee shop."

"Somehow I've never had the nerve to ask for a different table," I admitted. Denise was tapping her long fingernails against the menu, and her obvious nervousness was making me uneasy. We both ordered coffee and cheesecake, and I waited for her to speak. She said nothing for a long time.

"It's getting worse, Ruthie."

"Not another confrontation at the Stokes house?" I knew she'd been at work during the morning visit of Sheila and Scott, but perhaps they'd returned later.

The waitress brought our orders to the table, and we were quiet again. Denise looked down at her cheesecake and started mashing pieces of the crust, without eating anything. "I'm scared," she said suddenly.

My stomach tightened and I lowered the forkful of cake I'd just picked up. It looked like neither of us was going to eat anything tonight. "Why?"

"I lied to Detective Moreway."

"Are you sure you want to tell me this?"

"I have to tell someone," she said. "That Sunday night when Joey was killed, he called me just after midnight. His voice was strange. I didn't even realize it was Joey at first."

I stared at Denise. "You've got to tell the police he telephoned you. What did he say?"

"He said something was bothering him about Harry Stokes and he was trying to get answers."

"And what did he ask you? How long did you talk? It could narrow the time frame for the murder."

"You don't understand, Ruthie. He didn't tell me anything on the phone. He wanted me to meet him in front of the fountain."

"My God," I said. "You mean you were there?"

She must have realized how shocked I was. "You believe I did it. You think you're sitting here talking to a double murderer."

"I'm sure you realize it must be someone we know."

"So you suspect me. Well, I know I'm innocent, so maybe *I* should be suspicious of *you*."

I smiled uneasily. "I'm not the one who was at the fountain when Joey was killed."

"How do I know who else was there that night. But I do know Joey was expecting to meet someone after me."

"Tell me what happened," I said, hoping I could

put Denise's information together with everything I'd heard so far and figure out who the murderer was. After all, I knew all these people better than Frank Moreway did; I should be able to determine which one was lying. But I was too close to most of them. Denise was my friend, I worked with Tim, and I was—I guess emotionally involved was the best way to put it—with Michael and his daughter. I even sympathized with Sheila and Scott. With my personal feelings obscuring things, I would be hard-pressed to look at all of them dispassionately. The only one I'd disliked at once was Richard Stokes. How neatly it would tie together if Richard, who was going around accusing everyone else, had killed his father and Joey.

Denise had paused while the waitress refilled our coffee cups. She lifted her cup, and I did the same. I burned my tongue, and I wondered how she could drink it that hot. Then I noticed she didn't seem aware of the heat.

"Joey asked me if I thought it was murder if you gave someone a drug that was harmless to most people but not the one you gave it to."

"But that can describe so many medications," I said. "Maybe even all."

"I asked if it was done deliberately." She stared at me defiantly. "I guess I should apologize for getting angry at you a little while ago. The truth is, I thought Joey meant that he was the one who'd made a mistake."

This was a new angle, one I hadn't considered before. Could Harry Stokes have been killed in error? But if the mistake had been my technician's, who profited from Joey's own death?

"Who made the mistake?" I asked Denise.

"He didn't say it was a mistake."

"Then what did he say?" I was getting tired of people talking around the subject. If we were going to put the pieces together and solve the puzzle, we had to know all the details.

"He said he knew I used Food-Fed decongestant for

my allergies, and he wanted to know if I'd ever recommended them to Harry or given any to him."

"And?"

"I told him I never had." Her look was still defiant. "Whether you believe me or not, I had nothing to do with Harry's death."

"Do you think Joey was seeing all of the people who were close to Harry that night?"

"Why? Who else did he meet?"

I didn't want to tell her about Betsy and Michael, so I said nothing. But Denise wouldn't let it rest.

"Did he make an appointment with you?" she asked me.

That started another train of thought. If Joey was conducting an investigation of his own, why hadn't he called me, too? Did he think the error was mine? Maybe he intended to talk to me the next day but had been killed first.

Denise was waiting for my reply. "He did see others," I told her, "but it was before your appointment." I backtracked to something that was bothering me. "How is it the guard at the gate didn't see you?"

"No one was at the gate," she said. "I just drove right in, and about ten minutes later when we finished talking, I drove right out again."

"Did you park and get out of your car?"

"Ruthie, are you trying to trip me up? You've been there and you know there's no place to park by the fountain. I had to pull into the visitor's parking area and walk back to the fountain to talk to Joey."

"Weren't you afraid to be there alone at night?"

"I saw Joey waiting at the fountain as I drove in, and I certainly wasn't worried about him."

The coffee had cooled somewhat and I sipped it, wondering what else Denise had to reveal. She didn't wait for more questions, but continued in a high, excited voice. "He kept looking around, as if he thought someone might overhear us. But the place was deserted. Maybe he was watching in case the gate guard came along."

"And no one else showed up."

"No one. But we did hear a rustling noise about where the oleanders border the driveway."

"I suppose someone could have been hiding there. You wouldn't see anything even in the daytime."

"Joey got more nervous when we heard the noise. He wouldn't say another word."

Just what had happened at the Sizzler with Betsy and Michael, I thought. In a way, each of them had verified the other's story. If they were telling the truth, I reminded myself. And that would indicate that Joey had been seeing people all evening. Could the earlier ones be discounted as suspects, or did one of them decide Joey was too close to the truth and return to kill him?

"Ruthie, you've got to believe me," Denise said. "When I drove away, Joey was standing by the fountain. He must have been waiting for someone else."

"I don't suppose the real murderer would be telling me all this," I said, half to myself.

Denise seemed to relax and her voice lowered to its normal pitch. "Should I go to the police?"

My first impulse was to answer affirmatively. Even though I couldn't decipher the significance of Sunday night's events, the police had more experience with crime. They might see something that Denise and I were overlooking. But what if I advised her to go to Frank Moreway and he arrested her for murder?

"I really believe it's best to be honest with them, but there are no guarantees. It could be hard for you to prove Joey was alive when you left him."

"I'm not just being selfish," Denise insisted as if I'd accused her of it. "I keep thinking that if they concentrate on me again, the murderer might get away with it completely."

"Denise, everything we know about murder cases comes from newspaper stories and from fictional accounts in books and on television. Probably distorted in both cases. We need to let the people with real experience have all the facts. All the facts we're aware of," I amended.

She put her head in her hands and murmured something I couldn't hear, so I asked her to repeat it. "You still don't get it," she told me, lifting her head and staring fixedly at me.

All at once I did understand, because I could see the fear in her eyes. "I know it's a tough decision," I said, intending to comfort her.

"That's not it, Ruthie. The murderer saw me with Joey that night and may think I know too much. I'm afraid I'm in danger."

Twenty-two

I wanted to credit Denise's imagination with working overtime again, but thought about Joey. Suppose he had said the same words last week. Would anyone have believed him? It was time for amateurs like us to stop taking risks. Yet I was sure the answer lay in my prescription files, the files just about everyone had wanted to see. If I could figure out who the killer was, I could clear Denise from suspicion. And Michael most of all, I added, acknowledging in that moment how important he still was to me.

"Then you should go to Detective Moreway immediately," I told her firmly.

"That's easy advice, but I could get into a worse mess that way."

"Call it easy advice or whatever you want. It's the only sensible thing to do." I tried hard to convince Denise without letting her see that I was afraid, too. "Let's look at the worst case. If you go to the police and they jail you, at least you'll be alive and able to prove your innocence. But if the murderer really is after you, you won't get that chance."

Denise didn't respond, and I couldn't recognize any other emotion through the fear that still predominated. "I'll have to think about it," she said.

"Meanwhile, maybe it would be better if you tell me what you suspect. Did you catch a glimpse of the other person? Or see a familiar car when you parked yours? Did the noise you heard suggest who could have been there." I fired my questions at Denise, waiting for answers but getting only a shake of her head after each one.

"You can't exactly wear a signboard saying, 'I know nothing about it,'" I told her.

"Let's get out of here." She scooped her handbag and the check and started for the cash register. The cashier waited patiently while we added the tip and divided the check between us. Denise dropped all the loose change out of her wallet as we left the register and walked into the Village Inn parking lot.

Her nervousness was so obvious that I offered to help. "Why don't I follow behind you in my car?" I asked her. "I'll wait until you're safely inside the house?" Too bad neither one of us has a car phone, I thought. But I could make plenty of noise and rouse all Denise's neighbors if anything went wrong.

My offer seemed to calm her somewhat, but I saw her look into the backseat of her car before she opened the doors. I did the same with mine.

When we pulled into Denise's driveway, I watched carefully as she made her way inside. No one appeared to be around and about in her neighborhood. My own neighborhood was also quiet, with no lights showing at the Flints or the Woodmans when I arrived home. My hands were shaking when I unlocked the door leading from the garage into the kitchen.

The next day, Thursday, my schedule changed to the early shift. I found it hard to get started that morning. My beige- and coffee-colored print dress seemed lifeless, and I added a coral-and-gold necklace and matching earrings to feel more cheerful. I barely made it to Food Go to open on time, dreading what the day would bring, convinced I'd hear terrible news about Denise. The morning was a quiet one, and I was thankful for it. For once, customers and phone calls alike came one at a time. Before Tim arrived at two o'clock, I was completely caught up with my work.

I wondered if he'd refer to yesterday's conversation, but he mumbled a greeting and stationed himself at the computer. This was normal behavior for Tim, and I felt a surge of relief that he, at least, was acting the way he always did.

Denise didn't approach the pharmacy during her breaks, and I had neither breaks nor lunch hour to spend in the coffee shop, even if I had wanted to. When my shift was over, I debated with myself about heading there but went directly home instead.

I popped a frozen ravioli dinner in the microwave, quickly changed to my bathing suit, and jumped into the pool to cool down. It felt wonderful. I didn't even bother drying off but went right into my kitchen to turn the cardboard tray around in the microwave. During the remaining three minutes of cooking, I poured ice cubes into a glass and added a diet cola. Even when eating alone, I sometimes dressed the table with a pretty placemat and matching cloth napkin. Today I ate directly from the cardboard tray on a piece of paper towel. I felt like I was waiting for something to happen, but I didn't know what.

When the doorbell rang, I quickly threw a housedress over my bathing suit, and looked through the decorative glass inset of the front door. It was Detective Moreway. I felt a sharp twinge of fear at the sight of him, certain that something had happened to Denise.

He followed me into the kitchen and apologized for interrupting my dinner. Dinner hardly seemed the right word for the remaining bits of ravioli cooling in the cardboard microwave tray, sitting on a paper towel that was now spotted with tomato sauce. I was embarrassed but tried not to show it, offering Frank Moreway a can of diet cola, too. He asked for ice water instead.

I thought of all the detective stories I'd read in which the police refused drinks from suspects. Did ice water count, I wondered. On the other hand, it must still be over 105 degrees outdoors, and he looked as though he needed the ice water.

"Please finish your dinner," he said.

"I'm done," I told him as I scraped the remaining ravioli into the disposal and threw tray and towel into the trash container that I keep under my kitchen sink.

We both sat at the kitchen table. All the fizz had left my diet cola, but I drank it anyhow. The silence was unbearable, and I found it hard not to ask him what was uppermost in my mind.

"Were you off today or on an early shift?" he asked.

"You must have checked with the store before you came out here." That's a stupid answer, I thought. Why do you want to antagonize him?

"I'm asking because I did call the store, and they said you weren't there." I could tell he was making an effort to be patient.

"I was on the early shift, nine to four."

"And what about Mrs. Seaford? Was she at work today?"

"I didn't see her."

"And when did you see her last?"

"Yesterday." I hoped he would assume I'd seen her only at Food Go and wouldn't try to pin down the time, but he was persistent.

"Can you give me some details?"

I told him we'd gone out for coffee after work. It was not up to me to reveal our conversation. He listened carefully but wanted to know more.

"I understand Mrs. Seaford was on the day shift and came back to the store to meet you. Wasn't that unusual?"

"Not when you consider what's been happening."

"So her purpose was to talk about the murders?"

"Of course. We talk about them all the time. Isn't that normal?"

He didn't answer. "I also understand you were at the Stokes house yesterday before you went to work."

Now I was getting annoyed. "Are you following me around?"

"Why? Do you have something to hide?"

That remark angered me, but I forced myself to remain calm. "Tell me what this is all about, please. I can cooperate better if you don't play games with me."

"Suppose you give me a rundown of your visit to Betsy Stokes."

"You're still not revealing your reasons for these questions. I don't want to repeat private conversations without knowing what's going on."

"Will knowing my reasons change what you have to say?"

"No, but it will help me focus on what's important. I'm sure you don't want all the trivialities."

"I'll be the judge of that," he said, then relented enough to tell me that he wanted to hear about Sheila Stokes and Scott Robbins.

I wondered how he knew about their visit to Betsy and Michael. Or mine, for that matter. Perhaps he's already questioned some or all of the people involved, I thought. Five people had been present during the visit he was asking me about, and I supposed he would compare our stories. This must be the basis of police work. I nearly asked Frank Moreway if he'd ever seen *Rashomon,* the Japanese film in which each eyewitness gives a different version of the same crime. Could any group of people ever agree on what they'd seen and heard?

Although these reflections passed through my mind very quickly, they didn't solve my problem. I decided to be frank about Sheila and Scott's visit, omitting only Scott's accusation at the end.

Detective Moreway listened, taking notes from time to time. When I finished, his eyes held mine for a moment. "And what exactly did Scott say that caused Michael Loring to kick him out of the house?"

"He didn't kick Scott out," I said indignantly.

"Maybe not physically. But wouldn't you agree that

holding the door open until Scott and Sheila left was the psychological equivalent."

"They could have ignored him. It's not even his home."

"And if that led to physical action?"

"I don't understand what this is all about. Did Scott and Sheila file some sort of complaint? Are you trying to say that it's against the law to hint that you want unwelcome visitors to leave?"

"Mrs. Morris, you're evading the original question. I asked what Scott said directly before the confrontation."

"I don't remember," I said stubbornly.

Frank Moreway flipped back a few pages in his notebook. "I've been told Scott threatened to speak to me about Michael Loring. And he intended to claim that Michael killed Harry Stokes so Betsy could inherit."

He waited then, but I was silent. "Does that jog your memory?"

"Detective Moreway, everyone has been accusing everyone else. Either I ignore the accusations or I will never be able to trust my friends again."

"And is Michael Loring your friend?"

Another tough one. I decided to follow my advice to Denise and tell the truth. "We went to school together many, many years ago. Until recently, I hadn't seen him since that time."

I was afraid the next question would relate to the strength of that relationship, and who in today's society would believe Michael and I had not had an affair? But Frank Moreway changed the subject again.

"What vehicles do you own?"

The question was so unexpected, I hesitated for a fraction of a second. "I only own one car, a Honda Accord."

"Model year? Color?" He was writing in the notebook again.

"A ninety-one. White."

"What about your friend, Denise?"

I jumped up and rushed to his side of the table. "You must tell me what's wrong. What happened to Denise?"

"Just answer the questions, please."

"She drives a black Ford. An older one. I don't know the year."

"Does she have another vehicle?"

"Not that I know of."

He continued questioning me about other people and their cars. I remembered Michael's Lexus but had no idea what the others drove other than Scott, who had some kind of motorcycle. Then I recalled the Brandens had mentioned Richard Stokes's Mercedes, but this was not first-hand information. Again I asked what it was all about.

"Would you like to tell me why you're so concerned about Mrs. Seaford?"

"Because she's very nervous. I guess I picked up on that." I had no intention of revealing what Denise had told me last night at the restaurant. Thank God, no one else was present during that conversation.

"When did you first meet Scott Robbins?"

I was really bewildered now. His questions didn't seem to have any purpose. I wondered whether he was disorganized or trying to trip me up in some way.

"The first time I saw him was at the funeral. Harry Stokes's funeral. I didn't really meet him until yesterday."

"But Denise knows him well?"

"I have no idea."

"What about Michael Loring?"

"I've already said before that Michael turned up here the other week, and it had been years since I saw him." I knew my voice sounded plaintive, but the strain was beginning to show. No wonder they say people will confess to anything after relentless questioning.

I tried again. "Isn't it about time you told me why you're asking me these ridiculous questions about people's cars?"

"These aren't ridiculous questions, Mrs. Morris. Scott Robbins was seriously injured this morning. He was on his motorcycle; it was a hit and run."

Twenty-three

My first thought, relief that it wasn't Denise, was followed immediately by gratitude that I had been at work all morning. Dozens of customers and Food Go employees must have seen me there. Then I realized I didn't know the time of the accident.

"When did it happen?" I asked.

"Don't you want to know his condition?"

"Of course, I do. But the way you've been questioning me, I guess I want to be sure you don't suspect me."

"Nine-thirty this morning, near the university campus in Tempe. I suppose people can confirm you were in the pharmacy?"

He phrased it as a question, and I nodded my head in agreement. Knowing I was in the clear made me feel better than I had in days. Then I remembered his questions about the various vehicles other people owned.

"You think it was deliberate, not an accident," I said. Nothing else made sense in view of his questions.

"We don't know," he admitted.

Belatedly I asked about Scott's condition. "Will he be all right?"

"He might have been if the helmet law was still on the books. Right now, he's in intensive care. Head injuries."

I thought about Sheila, the caressing lilt to her voice when she called him "Scotty," and the way her eyes followed him. Not another widow to join the crowd, I hoped. But she would not be a widow in any case, at least not in the legal sense.

"Why would anyone want to run him down?" I asked.

"It isn't much more than twenty-four hours since he was accusing a specific person of murder. I'm not saying there's a connection, you understand, but we have to check into every possibility." He looked at the pages in his notebook again. "Will you confirm that Scott accused Michael Loring of murder yesterday?"

I remained quiet for a long time. Too long, but maybe he'd think I was trying to visualize the confrontation. "I don't remember," I repeated as firmly as I could.

"Let me help your memory," he said. "They were talking about money. About Sheila and her brother sharing in their father's estate. She wanted the money to start a business with her fiancé." Frank Moreway read from the notebook, "'I remember you from Tucson. You can't keep a job, Scott.'" He looked expectantly at me. "Do you remember those words?"

"Those weren't his exact words." Too late I realized I'd fallen into his trap.

"So, you do remember the conversation."

"Sheila's a lot younger than me. Her memory is probably better."

Detective Moreway laughed, and while his manner remained polite, it wasn't a pleasant sound. "Good excuse," he said. "In that case, assuming she's the source of my information, would you be willing to confirm the rest of it?"

"I can only tell you what I remember."

"Scott's words were addressed to Sheila." As Frank Moreway read them from his notebook, I hoped they'd be slightly off, too. Then I could honestly say I hadn't heard them. But Sheila, if she had been his informant, and I supposed she had to be the one, had been only too accurate. "'He probably killed your father so his own daughter would get all that money.'" Detective Moreway quoted.

Was it possible, I wondered. Thank God, the police were unaware that Michael had another strong motive, wanting to safeguard his daughter's expected baby. I was silent.

"We need your help," Frank Moreway said. "You can't protect people under a mistaken notion of friendship. If your friends are innocent, nothing you say will hurt them. But have you thought about the alternative? Are you willing to take a chance, even a slight chance, that you're shielding someone who's killed twice and is ready to kill again to protect himself or herself."

"If I knew anything to help you, I'd say it."

"How will you feel if someone else gets killed? I'm convinced you have information that could make the difference. Maybe not about the conversation that took place yesterday morning. You may not even be aware of the information you hold. But you know something." His eyes darkened as he stared intently at me. "You could be in danger, too," he told me.

I laughed uneasily. "You're trying to frighten me."

"And I hope I'm succeeding."

I remembered how nervous Denise had been the night before, convinced of her own danger. It wasn't pleasant to find myself in the same situation.

He was watching my face and must have understood my reaction. "If you have anything to add, now's the time."

I shook my head and he got up to leave. At the front door, he turned and told me to contact him when I changed my mind. He seems so sure of himself, I thought, as I locked up after him. But he couldn't be right. Whatever I knew, others knew as well. The murderer could gain nothing by coming after me.

Despite the air-conditioning, I felt uncomfortably hot and perspired. I was still in my bathing suit, so I removed my wraparound housedress and went out through the patio doors and into the pool to cool down. The swim calmed me only for a short time, and when I got out and dried off, I realized how agitated my thoughts were. I sat in front of the television the rest of the evening, but I don't remember what I watched, only that the local news had nothing about Scott Robbins and his motorcycle accident.

By morning I still had no thunderbolt of revelation. Maybe it was just too hot to think straight. Fridays were always busy because people wanted their medicines before the weekend. I was on the day shift again, and I was glad to keep occupied. Without a technician, it was even more difficult to keep up with the flow of customers. Luckily Greg Blackstone passed by when the lineup of people at the window was beginning to get out of control. He was a good manager, and immediately brought over one of the clerks from the film department. Karen was a high-school student, but she looked older. She was wearing shorts and a T-shirt, which wasn't good for the pharmacy's image, but I was desperate enough to appreciate any live body.

"Karen can help for a few hours," Greg told me. "What is she allowed to do?"

I explained to both of them that under my supervision, state law allowed her to take prescriptions from patients at the window. She could answer the telephone and write down the prescription number for a refill and the name of the person okaying it. But she must call me over for new prescriptions.

"I can see you're too busy to train Karen now," Greg said. "Isn't there something simple she can do to ease things for you?"

"Answering the phone would help most, Karen," I told her. "But call me over unless it's a refill."

"No problem," she said.

Although she seemed alert and happy to be away from the photo center, I was careful to keep tuned to the way she handled phone calls while I took care of everything else. Just having her to field the calls helped tremendously, and she needed no reminders to take down the numbers and prescribers' names. The first three calls were for refills, and I listened as I worked to see what would happen when a new script was called in.

"One minute, please," I heard her say. "The pharmacist will be right with you."

Maybe Greg would allow her to replace Joey, I thought. If she's computer literate, I can teach her our system, and she can enter information and do the labels. Then we can get to the more difficult tasks. Verifying the completeness of scripts, taking drugs off the shelves, counting or pouring. Joey had seemed to have a natural affinity for the pharmacy, and I remembered Mr. Franklin saying over and over that his son should have been a druggist. It was selfish to miss Joey because of his work in the pharmacy, but then again, I also missed his cheerfulness and his patience with customers.

Between phone calls, Karen asked if she could do anything else, and I soon had her at the window. She was polite and efficient and, after a while, wanted to hand out the finished prescriptions. I explained that state law didn't allow anyone but a registered pharmacist to do that.

"Why?" she asked. "If you're the one filling it, what difference does it make who gives it out?"

"I'm supposed to communicate with patients as I hand the medicine to them," I explained. "To tell them the name of the drug, its strength, the directions, and any cautions."

"Cautions?"

"Not to take it on an empty stomach or with milk products or that it might make them sleepy so they should try not to drive. Whatever they need to know to avoid problems."

She was listening to me wide-eyed, and I felt like some sort of guru. I remembered how fascinated I'd been at the same age when I helped in my Dad's drugstore. Fascinated enough to go to pharmacy college as soon as I finished high school.

Pharmacy college reminded me of Michael, and now, busy as I was, I could no longer postpone thinking of what I'd resolutely put out of my mind last night after Detective Moreway had left. Michael seemed to be the only one with a motive for trying to kill Scott Robbins. Scott had accused him of murder, and the next day, someone had gone after Scott. No matter how hard I tried to come up with another reason for the accident, nothing else fit. Combined with Michael's antipathy toward his son-in-law and evasions concerning his whereabouts on the night Joey died, this seemed like strong circumstantial evidence. I shut my eyes and tried to explain it all away, but I couldn't do it.

Somehow I got through the morning. For a person who'd always loved her work, I was finding it increasingly difficult to concentrate in the pharmacy. These days my mind was like a computer with insufficient disk space. And I couldn't seem to retrieve the data I needed.

Tim arrived at two o'clock and stared at Karen. "Are we running a kindergarten now?" he asked me, waiting until she was off the phone and couldn't miss hearing him.

"Karen's been invaluable, and if she's willing, I'm going to ask Greg if she can train as a technician."

"Fine, as long as you do the training."

Typical of Tim, I thought. He wanted to replace me as pharmacy manager but would never do any of the tasks that went with that job. Unfortunately I hadn't warned Karen about him, an awkward business anyhow. I couldn't denigrate a colleague to her, but I should have told her not to worry about his outward manner. A caution like those on prescription bottles!

Karen was on the telephone again, carefully taking down information about another refill. Since Tim had stationed himself in his usual position at the computer, I spent my time at the window, trying to catch up with paperwork whenever the flow of customers eased. I watched to see Karen's reaction to Tim's gruffness, but she simply avoided him as much as possible in the confined space of our small area. When she left to return to her own department, she agreed to put in as many hours in the pharmacy as Greg Blackstone allowed.

As soon as Karen was gone, I rounded on Tim. "You know we need a replacement for Joey. Please try to get along with her."

"I get along with everyone," Tim said.

To see ourselves as others do, I thought, and changed the subject. "Did you hear the latest about the killings?"

"They caught him?"

I was afraid to ask which "him" he meant. "No, it's something else. Scott Robbins was in a motorcycle accident. Hit and run."

Tim did an exaggerated double take. "Are you going to find connections between everything that happens to any of those people?" His skepticism showed in his voice and raised eyebrows.

"There is a relationship," I insisted.

"Sure," he said, with the same tone of disbelief.

I wasn't surprised. It was pointless to argue with Tim. His opinions were always the only right ones, so I don't know why I wanted to convince him. Maybe because I was avoiding Denise and needed to talk it over with someone.

We both got busy, but I was determined to continue the conversation. Since Tim's knowledge of Michael was more recent than mine, I had to find out what I could about the Michael Loring of today.

Just before my shift ended, we had another quiet spell and I brought the subject up again. "You may not believe it, but there's a definite chain of events." I didn't want to say anything about the conflicting reactions of Michael and Harry Stokes to Betsy's pregnancy, but I felt the pregnancy was an important factor.

"I think that chain begins with Betsy Stokes's visit to her obstetrician. You know I don't gossip about customers, but I think this is important. I keep going over the sequence in my mind. Betsy finds out she's pregnant. Next thing, her husband's dead. Maybe it's natural causes, maybe suicide, maybe murder. But then Joey, who works in the pharmacy where Betsy and Harry both get all their medications, is killed. And now Sheila Stokes's fiancé, a young man who knew most of the key players in Tucson, is seriously hurt in a hit and run." I said "key players" deliberately, to avoid mentioning Michael by name. I looked at Tim, wondering if he realized which key player I meant.

"You want to ramble on, it's okay with me. But what makes you think you're smarter than the police?"

"I never said that," I protested.

"Obviously, you have a suspect. Who is it? Betsy? Her father?"

He was getting too close now, and I didn't want to answer. But he persistently added names. "Harry's kids? Me? Denise?" He grinned at me. "What about you?"

"Now you're being ridiculous," I said.

"Why should you be any less of a suspect than anyone else?"

"And what's my motive?" I asked tartly, although I didn't mind the game if it led him away from Michael.

"Unrequited love."

I laughed uneasily. "For Joey or for Scott?"

"For the old man," he said and turned back to the computer screen, too quickly to see me wince at his words.

Don't be a fool, I told myself. To Tim, Harry Stokes *was* an old man, and the epithet helped him to belittle Betsy's choice. I wondered if I should tell him about my alibi for the time of Scott's accident, but decided his accusation hadn't been serious; there was no need to defend myself.

Although Tim was finished with the subject, I wasn't. Just before my shift ended, I began again. "Tim, you know these people better than I do. Seriously now, who do you think is responsible for what's going on?"

"I told you. Nothing is going on. You know as well as I do that Harry Stokes had all sorts of health problems. He died of natural causes."

"That's what we were supposed to think, but I know better."

His set expression showed his disagreement, but that didn't stop me because I was used to Tim taking the opposite point of view to mine on every possible occasion. "As for Scott," he went on, "do you know how many motorcyclists land in Tempe emergency rooms every day?"

I persisted. "And how will you explain away Joey's death?"

"That's easy. When you stop trying to connect three distinct events, Joey's death will turn out to be a mugging that went wrong. Or maybe a gang killing."

"If he'd been shot from a moving car rather than drowned, I might agree. But I don't believe in this kind of coincidence, and the way the police have been questioning all of us, I can see they don't either."

"What do they know?" he muttered and reached for the stack of new scripts I put next to the computer. I reminded him to transmit the order to the wholesaler before closing. To make sure he didn't forget again, I put the order machine where he couldn't miss it, and left for the day.

Sundown was more than two hours away, and it was at least 110 degrees outside. I'd been early enough to find a parking spot under a bottlebrush tree, and my car was hot but not unbearable. Even so, I was ready for a few laps in the pool before dinner.

Determined not to spend another agitated evening, I considered going to the movies. Only two weeks ago, I'd been at the mall with Denise and seen Michael for the first time since college. But I didn't want to call Denise even though I knew she probably had the same shift as I did today. As to my other friends, sometimes they included me in family outings, but I felt uncomfortable as the proverbial third wheel.

There was always television. It hadn't helped last night, but I turned on the set and mindlessly watched reruns for hours. At 9:30, I put on a dry bathing suit, turned on the patio lights, and went back to the pool. I was just drying off when someone knocked at the back gate.

This is such an early-to-bed city that I never expect late visitors. But it was Friday night and, although I had to work the next day, most people were off for the weekend. It must be Michael, I thought. A variety of emotions surged through my mind with that certainty. I wanted to see him again, but would it be safe to open the gate for him? I reminded myself that this was Michael, the man I had nearly married. Wrapping the huge beach towel over my bathing suit, sarong fashion, I walked over to the gate and looked out. I was surprised to see Tim but somewhat relieved that it wasn't Michael.

"I tried telephoning, Ruthie, but no one answered."

"It's hard to hear the phone when I'm swimming," I explained as I unlocked the gate. "What's happening?"

"I need your advice about a strange conversation I had with Greg Blackstone tonight. He sounded like he's ready to transfer me."

This was surprising. I couldn't remember Tim ever asking my advice before. In any case, I was glad to have this opportunity for a talk with him away from the busy pharmacy. Our conversations in the store had left me edgy because I couldn't shake the feeling that some things he'd said should be followed up and clarified.

Tim sat at the glass-topped patio table across from me and refused my offer of iced tea, while I thought about this development. I'd been hoping for months that Tim would transfer out. From a selfish point of view, this wasn't the right time because I'd have a new technician and a new staff pharmacist to contend with simultaneously. Surely Greg was aware of this problem, so why would he suddenly try to send Tim to another Food Go store? I wondered if Karen had complained to the manager about him.

"If you want to make a change, I wouldn't stand in your way," I told Tim, giving him a chance to put a positive spin on the transfer. Now I sound like a politician, I thought. Why does Tim always make me feel like the old-fashioned, stereotypical female boss?

"You were asking me about Betsy Loring tonight," he said. "Why?"

"Why?" I echoed and hesitated. I certainly was not going to tell him my suspicions about Michael.

We heard the click as my pool cleaning system started up. I realized it was ten o'clock, the hour I'd set the timer for. Tim stood and sauntered over to the pool. "What kind of cleaner is that, anyhow?"

It was an odd change of subject, but I was used to friends watching my little robotic system in action. I walked over and joined him, ready to point out the pros and cons of the new pool cleaner, wondering why I felt so uneasy. Suddenly I knew, but my mind didn't recognize the danger for a second or two. And before I could react, Tim grabbed me and edged me closer to the pool. Without consciously reasoning it out, I understood they would find me floating facedown in that swimming pool unless I acted quickly. Tim was younger and stronger than I, but I was determined to save myself.

Twenty-four

He was dragging me along the pebbled decking to the deep end of the pool, and I foolishly wondered why he didn't simply hold my head under water at the shallow part. But this time he has to be sure it looks like an accident, I realized. He can't drown me in shallow water, and he can't leave any unexplained marks on me. That must be why he isn't trying to choke me.

He was behind me, one hand over my mouth to keep me from screaming, the other wrapped around my abdomen, inexorably forcing me closer and closer to the deep end. My arms were free, but I couldn't reach him, even if I had the strength to fight him. I remembered reading about protesters who went limp to make their bodies more difficult to drag, and I tried to deaden my weight. If only I had the Mace spray now. It probably wouldn't stop him for long, but it could buy me enough time to get out of the gate and over to Jean and Jerry's house.

The spray would be where I always put it when I swam, on the stone bench alongside the pool, next to my bathing cap and swim goggles. I couldn't tell if we'd already passed the bench, but as I reached my hand out to check, I felt my legs scrape along its base. This was my only chance, and I was going to make the most of it. My heartbeat speeded up as I got ready to grab the canister, lift it in Tim's direction, and squeeze the nozzle before he realized what was happening. I also had to expect the spray to affect me but, I hoped, not as severely as it would Tim.

As all this flashed through my mind, I felt my bathing cap on the bench and was afraid I'd passed by the Mace. But I wasn't going to give up. A fraction of a second later, I had the canister in my hand, aimed it behind me, and pressed. We were both coughing, but the attack shocked Tim long enough to cause him to slacken his hold on me. I ran to the gate, released the spring lock, and was out in the driveway so quickly that I hadn't even decided where to go. I only knew I needed help, and I could hear myself screaming for it as strongly as I could between bouts of coughing.

No one will hear, I thought in despair. They'll all be watching television or sleeping. I didn't dare look back to see whether Tim had recovered enough to come after me. Then I heard the gate click and knew he was close behind. Someone grabbed my arms and I screamed loud enough to bruise my throat before I realized it couldn't be Tim. This person was in front of me, and he let go immediately.

"Ruthie, it's all right. You're safe."

It was Michael's voice, and I stopped screaming although I still couldn't stop the ragged coughing. There were no racing footsteps behind us. "Tim," I said. "He's trying to kill me."

"Yes, but he may as well give up," Michael said, shouting so Tim would hear him. "I called the police on my car phone as soon as I saw his car in your driveway."

Michael's Lexus was slanted across the driveway, blocking Tim's green Riviera. We couldn't see Tim, but we could hear him coughing. The sound told us he was running across my lawn to the street. "He can't get far," Michael said. "I'll let the police be the heroes."

We heard the sirens then. Within minutes, two Scottsdale patrol cars pulled into the driveway. Somehow, because he was so closely connected in my mind with the investigation, I expected to see Frank Moreway. But I didn't recognize any of the four patrol officers who approached us, and I was afraid we'd waste valuable time explaining while Tim got away.

Michael immediately called to them that he was the one who had telephoned, and I vouched for him. We pointed out the direction Tim had taken. One officer stayed behind to talk to us.

Before I could begin my story, my legs started to shake so violently that I had to sit on the grass at the side of my driveway. Michael sat beside me, offering his shoulder for support.

After my first few sentences, the officer left us and went back to his patrol car to use the radio. And by the time I finished telling him exactly what had happened, another patrol car pulled up. Detective Moreway got out.

By this time, too, the Flints, the Woodmans, and other neighbors had gathered on the sidewalk in front of my house. I wondered why the arrival of the police had brought them out but not my screams. Then again, I could be misjudging them; they could have waited just inside their front doors, ready to provide a haven for me.

I'd always preferred neighbors who minded their own business, but perhaps it was better to have people like the Brandens living next door. They would have been outside at the sound of my first scream. None of this matters, I thought soberly. If I hadn't reached the canister of Mace on my own, it would have been too late.

I expected to see the police hauling Tim to one of the patrol cars by now, but they returned without him. One of them must have radioed for the police helicopter, for it was soon overhead spotlighting the area. Local television and newspaper reporters soon arrived on the scene. I didn't want to talk or allow them into the pool area, but I didn't have the strength to resist. Denise told me later that she saw me on the morning news, sitting on my front lawn, wearing only a pink bathing suit. That must have been a sight, a fifty-five-year-old pinup.

The questions and the commotion finally stopped. One patrol car remained outside the house, and the two police officers in it assured me I was safe. The front door was still locked. There was no way Tim could have passed us and reached the back door through the driveway. Michael checked out the house anyhow and poured a glass of Mogen David wine for me, the only alcoholic beverage I had in the house.

"I'm going to leave now, Ruthie. Lock up after me, get some rest, and we'll talk in the morning."

As he spoke, an idea struck with the force of a blow to the head. "Michael, I forgot. Betsy is the key to everything. He could go after her." I was pulling at his arm, trying to make sure he understood. "You've got to call and warn her not to open the door for him."

I didn't know how much time had elapsed since Tim's escape, but since his car was still in my driveway, he couldn't have reached the Stokes's home quickly. Michael's face paled and he ran to my kitchen phone. He gripped the receiver fiercely as he waited. The phone rang unanswered for a long time, and his grim expression haunted me. When she picked up the phone, he started to relax but I saw his brows knit as he talked to her.

"Are you alone, Betsy?"

He waited, tension in every line of his face. Then the lines softened, but he warned her not to let Tim Barnard in the house no matter what excuses he gave her.

She must have wanted reasons, because I heard him explain that Tim had just tried to kill me. "I'll be there as quickly as possible," Michael said and hung up the telephone.

"Can't we get the police to watch her house, too?"

"It will take too long to convince them. I've got to be there myself."

"Call those neighbors," I told him. "The Brandens. They can keep watch until you arrive. No, you go. I'll call them. Will you phone me when you get there?"

He nodded and dashed to the front door, stopping only long enough to be sure I locked up behind him. I tried unsuccessfully to reach the Brandens, wishing I'd thought about the danger to Betsy earlier.

If the police hadn't been busy trying to capture Tim, Michael would surely have gotten a ticket for speeding. I watched him from my dining-room window as he shot out of the driveway and raced up the street. Then there was silence. The neighbors had drifted away and so had the reporters, and the men in the remaining patrol car were quiet shadows.

I waited for Michael's call. It should take him about twenty minutes to drive to his daughter's home, maybe only fifteen the way he was going. When he hadn't called at the end of half an hour, I began to worry.

My thoughts were wild. What if Tim had been lurking at Betsy's and used her father as a hostage to get into the house? I paced from room to room, holding my portable phone so I could answer the instant Michael's call came through.

All the news items I'd ever seen about rejected lovers who killed family, friends, and anyone else they blamed for the breakup flashed through my mind. I realized I couldn't bear the thought of losing Michael and couldn't believe I had ever suspected him of murder. During these few weeks, I had grown used to his warm smile and vibrant personality again. Even if we were only to remain friends and see each other occasionally, that would be enough for me. And surely he'd call now and then when he came up to Scottsdale to see Betsy and his grandchild. With all my foolish suspicions behind us, we could reminisce lightheartedly and enjoy each other's company.

I continued to pace, wondering if I should go outside to the patrol car and ask them to check on the

Stokeses' house. Michael had always been dependable. Surely he couldn't have forgotten to call and reassure me that his daughter was safe.

Just as I made up my mind to approach the police, the phone rang. At Michael's "Hello, Ruthie," I sat on the floor right where I was and leaned against the wall, weak with relief.

"I'm sorry for the delay," he said. "We had some excitement here, but we're both okay."

"Tim was there?" I could barely get the question out. "He was at Betsy's house?" I remembered the terror of that scene by my swimming pool and grieved at the thought of a pregnant young woman going through similar violence.

"He was hiding by the front door, behind one of the pillars. I was unlocking the door, when he came up and tried to force his way into the house."

I was glad I had the wall for support. It was too easy to imagine the scene as Michael described it.

"Luckily I was able to reverse direction and back into him," Michael continued. "We both landed on the walk and had a bit of a fight, but it didn't last long. I was so furious with him for trying to kill you and for going after Betsy, that the police had to pry me off him when they arrived."

"Are you really all right?" I asked, my voice shaky with relief that Tim must now be in police custody.

"Absolutely. Would you believe Betsy had gone back to bed after my call from your place and slept through it all?"

"Then who called the police?" I asked. But I knew my earlier conjecture about neighbors like the Brandens was accurate.

Michael gave me a few more details about Tim's arrest. "They'll probably recall the patrol car at your house," he said. "Do you think you'll be all right?"

I assured him that I'd be fine and repeated my assurances to the officer who came to the door to tell me what I already knew about Tim's arrest. But even though I knew I was safe, I spent what was left of that night with my canister of Mace on the pillow next to me.

Twenty-five

It would have been wonderful to stay home the next day, but that was my Saturday on. Even if it were my day off, though, they'd have needed me to open up the pharmacy, because Tim would never be available again.

I had to force myself to shower and dress. Breakfast was out of the question, but I finally got into my car, wilted from monsoon humidity in the brief interval before the air-conditioning kicked in. By the time I arrived at Food Go, I didn't know how I'd make it through the day.

Greg Blackmore, who'd heard the news on his car radio, was waiting for me at the pharmacy. "Fill me in, Ruthie. I can't believe what they're saying about Tim Barnard."

"It's true. He tried to drown me last night."

Greg's usually placid expression creased into a rubbery mask of horror, but before I could give him details, my first customer of the day approached the window with three prescriptions in her outstretched hand. "I don't think you should be working today," Greg said as he walked away. "Call around and see if you can get someone to fill in."

Coming from my store manager, this request meant I could have the day off, provided I found a replacement. Before taking care of customers—they were now starting to line up—I got on the telephone, searching for an available relief pharmacist. Luck was with me. I made contact with a recent pharmacy graduate, Louise Rettenberg, who was working as a floater for Food Go, filling in where needed. She had nothing scheduled and would be there within the hour.

Greg sent Karen to work in the pharmacy, and I was energized enough to take care of all the waiting customers before Louise arrived. She was a little shorter than me, with dark hair that she wore in one neat braid. It reached just below the back collar of her store jacket. I was pleased to see her shake hands with Karen when I introduced them. Some pharmacists are condescending toward technicians, which destroys the harmony in our small workspace. If Louise is willing to work full time, I thought, maybe she can replace Tim.

Even though she was familiar with the basic Food Go layout and methods, I spent some time showing Louise the peculiarities of our pharmacy. Since Karen was also new, I didn't feel I could leave right away, but at least the pressure had eased for me.

Just as I was preparing to hand over to Louise, I looked up to see Betsy and Michael at the window. "I hoped you'd be home today, resting up after your ordeal," Michael said.

"It's arranged now," I told him. "I'm about to go."

"We're all meeting in the coffee shop," Betsy said. "Will you join us?"

If I'd given any thought to the people she included, I would have guessed at Denise, so I wasn't surprised to see her when we walked into the coffee shop. The others, sitting where Denise had moved two tables together, were the unexpected ones. Richard Stokes and his wife, Nancy, sat across from Sheila and Denise. Verna and Raymond Branden were at the other table, and Michael held out chairs at that table for his daughter and me. He carried over another chair, placed it at one end of the joined tables, and sat with us.

No one spoke. Ellen, the waitress on duty, took our orders. The others wanted only coffee, but I suddenly realized I was starving and asked for French toast and iced tea. We waited silently for our orders and when they came, Michael gave me just enough time to cut the French toast into bite-sized pieces and eat one or two of them.

"Ruthie, we all need to know what happened," Michael said. "Not just last night, but what led up to it. I thought I was dangling myself as bait to catch the killer, and all the time, you were the one in danger."

Richard spoke up, too, sounding no less petulant now that he knew none of those present had harmed his father. "I don't even know that guy. How did he get into the picture?"

I was too tired to match clichés with him again. "Betsy or Michael can tell you about that."

"Tim and I used to date before I met your Dad," Betsy told him. "He was possessive. I guess that's the best word. He didn't want me to go anywhere or do anything without him, not even with the friends I grew up with."

"I never liked the way he treated Betsy," Michael added. "But I didn't recognize that he was dangerous."

"He could have killed all of us," Richard said. "You should have warned us about him."

We all looked at Richard, wondering if he would ever understand. His sister put her hand on his arm. "Do you think Michael would have endangered his daughter if he'd suspected anything?"

"Not everyone who shouts is dangerous," Nancy Stokes said. We all understood she was referring to her husband, although it wasn't clear whether he realized it.

"I moved up from Tucson to get away from Tim," Betsy continued. "It took him a few months to find me. One of my friends who didn't know about our problems gave him the address."

"And meanwhile you met Dad," Sheila said.

"Yes, meanwhile I met Harry." Betsy's voice had softened. "He seemed so safe. And self-confident enough not to be possessive. The opposite of Tim in every way."

"You really did care for Dad." Sheila's voice held a note of surprise.

"Sheila," Richard said warningly.

"Oh, give it up. Betsy and I have both been through enough." Sheila turned to Betsy. "I didn't understand what it was like for you until I nearly lost Scott. I'm sorry for adding to your unhappiness."

Betsy nodded her thanks and continued. "When Tim first found me, I told him it was over. He didn't believe it." She turned to me. "That's why he transferred from Food Go in Tucson and moved up here."

"But that must have been at least a year ago," Denise said. "Before you married. I don't understand why Tim waited so long to kill Harry."

"That's why Betsy and I never suspected him," Michael said. "He seemed to change, to want to be a friend; he never threatened her or Harry."

Betsy's face reddened slightly. "He'd convinced himself that it was nothing personal, that I married Harry for his money. I don't know what changed his mind about that."

It was time for me to explain, but I asked for Betsy's permission before I talked about her prescriptions. "Everyone's been asking the wrong question all along," I told her. "Detective Moreway, your Dad, Richard. All of them wanted to know what prescriptions the various people in the Stokes family were taking."

"That was the wrong question?" Richard's voice was surprisingly quiet.

"Yes, the question should have been, 'Who knew what medicines all of you were taking?'" I turned to Betsy again. "When you went to your obstetrician and learned you were pregnant, you came here with the prescription for Stuartnatal 1 + 1, the prenatal vitamin. That was on July eighteenth, a Saturday. It was my day off, and Tim filled your prescription."

"How do you know that?" Richard demanded.

"His initials were on the computerized record. I never gave it a thought, but Tim knew immediately what that prescription meant. Until your pregnancy, he could convince himself he was a self-sacrificing lover. He even told me he'd 'agreed' to a marriage of convenience so Betsy could have all the material things she deserved."

"That's just what he said when he met Harry last year," Betsy said.

"Tim had no trouble believing you still loved him. In his eyes, Harry was an old man and no threat. Maybe Tim thought you'd come back to him one day. The baby changed all that. It probably made the marriage real for the first time. I'm convinced that's what drove him over the line."

"He never said anything to me," Betsy told us. "We'd known each other for so many years, I was foolish enough to think he'd congratulate me. That young man took the written prescription from me. Joey, the one who was killed. I could see Tim by the computer, but he never came over to the window."

"He must have handed you the filled prescription," I said.

"No, Joey brought it to me. Tim just stood there and never even glanced up."

Michael and I looked at each other. We were the only ones there who knew that Arizona law required the pharmacist, not the technician, to physically give the script to the patient. Well, that was the least of Tim's legal incursions.

"So Joey knew something was strange even then," I mused aloud.

"Surely Tim didn't risk killing him just for that," Michael said.

"No. But Betsy caught the summer cold that was going around and a week later, she brought in prescriptions for a cough mixture, Tussi-Organidin DM, and for penicillin."

"He talked to me that time," Betsy said. "My throat was sore, I was terribly congested, and I was coughing. Tim seemed very sympathetic and recommended the Food-Fed decongestant." She thought for a moment. "He even asked after Harry."

"Did he ask whether Harry was sick, too?"

"Yes, he did."

"That must have been when the idea first took shape in Tim's mind," I said. "Harry filled all his prescriptions here, so Tim knew Harry had high blood pressure and diabetes, and that it was dangerous for him to take decongestants. All he had to do was wait for Harry to come in and recommend that he take his wife's Food-Fed."

"But surely that's not a foolproof way to kill someone," Raymond Branden said.

"No, not guaranteed, but Tim knew if it worked, no one could ever prove foul play. And when Harry came in on the twenty-seventh, he had new prescriptions—increased dosages for his high blood pressure and diabetes medicines."

"Yes." Betsy's voice had a tinge of sadness. "He was so upset emotionally because of the baby and our arguments, it must have thrown him off balance physically as well."

"Your dad and I discussed all of this before, but we were looking at it from the wrong angle." I wasn't going to admit that, like the police, I'd suspected Betsy of giving the decongestants to her husband. Her eyes met mine and I could see she understood.

"But why did Tim kill Joey?" Denise asked. "And why did he go after you?"

"It would have been a perfect crime if he stopped after Harry's death," I said. "But Joey was a bright young man who wanted to go to medical school. He was always asking questions and reading package inserts." At the Brandens' blank looks, I explained that package inserts are information sheets that tell all about the drug and its possible side effects.

"Joey knew more about medicine than most pharmacy technicians," I continued. "He would have realized something was wrong when Tim wouldn't hand Betsy's prescriptions to her and didn't discuss the drugs with her. But we were both accustomed to Tim's attitude problems. Joey would have known the omission was illegal, but I doubt if he gave it much thought at that point."

"Then why did Joey want to see Denise and my dad?" Betsy asked.

"We know Joey was aware of the various precautions for different drugs. He certainly heard us talk to patients over and over during the two years he worked at Food Go. And he always asked why some drugs couldn't be taken with others. Joey's parents told me something was bothering him after Harry's death, something that affected his eating and sleeping habits. He must have heard Tim recommend the Food-Fed, and it must have been on his mind."

"If Joey hadn't been killed, I'd suspect he was the one who recommended the decongestant and that he did it by mistake," Michael said.

"Impossible," I told him. "The first month Joey worked here, he would suggest over-the-counter remedies for customers. I caught him at it and warned him never to do that again. He argued with me, complaining that I underestimated him, that he only recommended drugs he was familiar with. I had to explain the state pharmacy board's views on consultations to him. And I told him, even *I* don't recommend specific over-the-counter drugs because we can be sued if something goes wrong. I always show customers where things are and name two or three possibilities. And then I advise them to check with their physicians."

"And did that little lecture stop Joey?" Michael asked with a smile.

"After he heard it two or three times, yes. It's a long

time since Joey did anything of the sort, and I'm sure he didn't with Harry."

"Besides," Sheila said. "If the recommendation to take that decongestant came from Joey, he'd still be alive."

Richard was ready to argue again. "Only if you assume my father's and Joey's deaths were connected."

"I admit it's an assumption," I told him. "But remember the night Joey was killed, he had met with most of the principals in this case. I think it's a valid assumption that he saw Tim, too."

"But why did that awful man try to kill Scott and then you?" Nancy Stokes spoke up for the first time. I saw her husband glare at her and watched her shrink back in her seat. But the question had been asked, and despite Richard's reaction to his wife's mild attempt at independence, I was going to answer her.

"My questions about his relationship with Betsy and his feelings when she married someone else were getting too close. I even told him I was convinced Betsy's pregnancy had initiated the chain of events. Then he slipped up when he claimed to have heard nothing about Scott but knew the accident happened in Tempe. I didn't realize it at the time, but he must have figured I would remember his words later on. So he came to my house to see how much I really knew. He might have left without the attempt on my life." I looked apologetically at Betsy. "But I hesitated when he tried to find out the reason for my questions about you."

"And Scott?" Nancy asked again.

"Scotty regained consciousness this morning," Sheila told her. "He's not thinking too clearly yet. But he confirmed that when Betsy first left Tucson, Tim had threatened to get anyone who took his place in her life."

"I wish I'd known that," I said.

"You wouldn't have wasted time suspecting me," Michael said.

Startled, I turned too quickly toward him, giving myself away. But his eyes had that teasing brightness I remembered so well. I managed a light smile, embarrassed at being understood.

"Detective Moreway told me about your lapse of memory," Michael continued. The others looked puzzled, but neither one of us explained.

"The part that bothers me," I said, "is having to get the details from TV and the papers. In books, the police come around and wrap up everything for the participants."

"You expected Tim to confess?" Betsy asked.

"I don't know what I expected, but it feels unfinished."

"Tim will never admit he's wrong about anything. The police will have to rely on your testimony and on Scott's."

"But that's only *attempted* murder." I could hear the dismay in Denise's voice. "Harry and Joey deserve vengeance."

Everyone was quiet. I know I was thinking how doubtful it was that Tim would ever be implicated in Harry's death. But there was Joey, and Detective Frank Moreway was married to his sister. "Don't worry," I assured Denise. "Now that the police know where to look, they'll surely find evidence linking Tim to Joey's murder."

This seemed the signal to break up. The Brandens were the first to leave, and then Richard pulled his wife away without saying goodbye. Sheila shook hands with the rest of us, and I was pleased to hear the warmth in her voice when she told Betsy she'd call soon.

After a few awkward moments while Michael picked up the check and paid at the register, Denise said she'd better be clocking in for work. Betsy and I stood in the doorway of the Food Go coffee shop.

"I want to thank you, Ruthie. Dad told me you were the one who realized I might be in danger last night."

"We were both lucky."

She smiled at me with that same sweet expression I'd first noticed at her house a few days before. Then she looked toward her father, who was approaching the doorway. "Dad, let me have your car keys, and I'll get the air-conditioning started."

We both looked after Betsy as she walked out into the Food Go parking lot. "I think she'll be all right now," I said.

"Yes," Michael agreed. "But I'll be coming up from Tucson every few weeks to check on her." He took my hand and the blue eyes looked steadily at me. "And on you, too," he said.

Murder Is on the Menu at the Hillside Manor Inn

Bed-and-Breakfast Mysteries by
MARY DAHEIM
featuring Judith McMonigle

BANTAM OF THE OPERA
76934-4/ $5.50 US/ $7.50 Can

JUST DESSERTS
76295-1/ $5.99 US/ $7.99 Can

FOWL PREY
76296-X/ 5.50 US/ $7.50 Can

HOLY TERRORS
76297-8/ $5.50 US/ $7.50 Can

DUNE TO DEATH
76933-6/ $5.50 US/ $7.50 Can

A FIT OF TEMPERA
77490-9/ $4.99 US/ $5.99 Can

MAJOR VICES
77491-7/ $4.99 US/ $5.99 Can

MURDER, MY SUITE
77877-7/ $5.99 US/ $7.99 Can

Buy these books at your local bookstore or use this coupon for ordering:

Mail to: Avon Books, Dept BP, Box 767, Rte 2, Dresden, TN 38225   E
Please send me the book(s) I have checked above.
❏ My check or money order—no cash or CODs please—for $_____ is enclosed (please add $1.50 per order to cover postage and handling—Canadian residents add 7% GST).
❏ Charge my VISA/MC Acct#_____Exp Date_____
Minimum credit card order is two books or $7.50 (please add postage and handling charge of $1.50 per order—Canadian residents add 7% GST). For faster service, call 1-800-762-0779. Residents of Tennessee, please call 1-800-633-1607. Prices and numbers are subject to change without notice. Please allow six to eight weeks for delivery.

Name_____
Address_____
City_____State/Zip_____
Telephone No._____   DAH 0896

Faith Fairchild Mysteries by Agatha Award-Winning Author
Katherine Hall Page

THE BODY IN THE CAST
72338-7/$5.99 US/$7.99 Can

THE BODY IN THE VESTIBULE
72097-5/ $5.99 US/ $7.99 Can

THE BODY IN THE BOUILLON
71896-0/ $5.99 US/ $7.99 Can

THE BODY IN THE KELP
71329-2/ $5.99 US/ $7.99 Can

THE BODY IN THE BELFRY
71328-4/ $5.50 US/ $7.50 Can

THE BODY IN THE BASEMENT
72339-5/ $4.99 US/ $6.99 Can

Buy these books at your local bookstore or use this coupon for ordering:

Mail to: Avon Books, Dept BP, Box 767, Rte 2, Dresden, TN 38225   E
Please send me the book(s) I have checked above.
❏ My check or money order—no cash or CODs please—for $_____ is enclosed (please add $1.50 per order to cover postage and handling—Canadian residents add 7% GST).
❏ Charge my VISA/MC Acct#_____ Exp Date_____
Minimum credit card order is two books or $7.50 (please add postage and handling charge of $1.50 per order—Canadian residents add 7% GST). For faster service, call 1-800-762-0779. Residents of Tennessee, please call 1-800-633-1607. Prices and numbers are subject to change without notice. Please allow six to eight weeks for delivery.

Name_____
Address_____
City_____State/Zip_____
Telephone No._____   KHP 0896